"Are you coming?" Carly asked

Hunt bit his tongue and caught up to her in a few easy strides. He jumped into the soft sand that led down to the surf, but she remained behind.

"I'm going back," she said.

"We just got here. And it looks like the perfect night for a swim."

She crossed her arms. "I'm not wearing my bathing suit."

"Don't tell me you've never skinny-dipped."

"I leave that one to your imagination," Carly said. "And now you're staring."

"Not staring—imagining." Hunt's eyes lingered on her legs and continued a slow, upward travel until his gaze met hers. "I'm going in," he said, tossing his T-shirt toward her, shedding his pants. "And if you're the woman I think you are... you'll be right behind me."

Blaze™

Dear Reader,

Coming Undone is a very special book for me—it's my first Harlequin Blaze novel. I'm thrilled to be able to bring you Hunt and Carly's story!

My working title for this book was *Over the Falls*, which is a surfing term that literally means to lose control. I wanted to explore that theme with a hero and heroine who were both strong enough to handle anything life threw at them. Carly, a former pro surfer who's having some trouble getting back on her board, and Hunt, a navy SEAL who decides he's going to help Carly experience her fantasies both in and out of the water, absolutely lived up to that challenge, and then some.

I'd love you to lose yourself in *Coming Undone!*

All best,

Stephanie

COMING
UNDONE
Stephanie Tyler

HARLEQUIN®

TORONTO • NEW YORK • LONDON
AMSTERDAM • PARIS • SYDNEY • HAMBURG
STOCKHOLM • ATHENS • TOKYO • MILAN • MADRID
PRAGUE • WARSAW • BUDAPEST • AUCKLAND

ISBN-13: 978-0-373-79319-8
ISBN-10:   0-373-79319-7

COMING UNDONE

This edition published by arrangement with Harlequin Books S.A.

® and TM are trademarks of the publisher. Trademarks indicated with
® are registered in the United States Patent and Trademark Office, the
Canadian Trade Marks Office and in other countries.

www.eHarlequin.com

Printed in U.S.A.

For my daughter Lily,
who is my very favorite surfer girl and
who has more courage than anyone I know.

1

"I STARTED WITH, I THINK it's sexy when we cuddle."

At her best friend's words, Carly tried hard not to laugh into the phone's receiver, but she was unsuccessful. Cuddling was not sexy. Cuddling was for dogs and cats; it wasn't appropriate fantasy material. Not the erotic kind, anyway, which is what Samantha had attempted to write for her boyfriend.

Carly sat back in her chair and tried to compose herself. After a minute, she managed to choke out, "Sam, I don't think cuddling's going to get Joe all hot and bothered. Telling him that you want to cuddle *after* he strips off your clothes slowly, gets you spread-eagled on the bed and has his way with you thoroughly might get him revved up. But you'd have to be more explicit. You could start with something like, I want to feel your tongue tracing a path down my neck, while your hand reaches between my…"

"Ha. I'm surprised you remember what a man's touching you is like."

"Why are we friends again?" Sam's easy laughter made Carly smile into the phone.

"Because I'm here to remind you that you need to get back to your wild ways. Mainly so I can live vicariously through you," Sam said.

"It's time for *you* to get a little wild. Let yourself go and try again. Joe will love it."

The inspiration for her friend's truly awful creation was an article in *Total Woman Magazine,* written by Candy

Valentine, titled: "Take Him Over The Falls: Revealing Your Most Erotic Fantasy To Your Man."

Sam had lent her the magazine last week, and Carly had had a good chuckle over the title of the piece, an old surfing term that literally meant losing control. Apparently, the article had started some kind of erotic fantasy-writing craze, and her best friend had decided to jump on the bandwagon.

The article had given Carly food for thought. Lots and lots of thought.

"I'm not good at this kind of stuff," Sam said.

"You're confusing sexual fantasy with romance. They're very different animals, according to Candy. You've got to forget the cozy-up by the fire routine and think about turning up the heat from the inside instead," Carly explained.

"Obviously it's something I'm not accomplishing in real life or on paper."

The hurt in her friend's voice was clear. Carly knew that Samantha and her boyfriend of a few months had hit a snag in the bedroom department.

Personally, Carly thought Joe was less than deserving of her friend, but she had to admit Samantha *was* slightly puritanical in her views on sex. If Carly could get her to loosen up, maybe she'd see that there was more to life than Joe.

Of course, this was coming from someone who hadn't had a date in months, let alone anything close to a relationship, and she didn't plan on changing that status anytime soon. "Maybe the problem's not you, Sam."

"Maybe, but I'm willing to give this a shot. Hey, are you ready for your parents' visit?"

"Yes, and a root canal without Novocain."

"More wedding talk, right? And you still don't have a date."

"Don't remind me." Carly pinched the bridge of her nose at the thought of how *not* well the visit was about to go. "And I have got an article due for the magazine, and the charity event's coming up—"

"I'll make you a deal. If you start the fantasy for me, I'll help you with the event," Samantha offered.

"Fine. I'll start it, but you'll have to finish it." Carly knew she could use the help to plan her part of the charity event. And she'd known she was going to help Sam fix her writing from the second she'd heard that woeful attempt. "Let me get myself into fantasy mode and I'll e-mail it to you in a while."

"My computer's down. Fax it instead. And don't let your parents see it."

"Don't even joke about that." She could imagine what her mother would say if she caught her eldest daughter writing erotic fantasies.

Women, especially women who were born into society, as her mother often termed it, weren't supposed to have fantasies. Women with Carly's social standing were to marry well, have children, work for various charities and generally do all things ladylike.

She had no problem with the charities per se, especially since her family had a legacy of service to the community, beginning with her great-grandmother and continuing into the present, thanks to her mother's pageant work. Except the event her mother had volunteered Carly for truly inspired mixed feelings, ones she was trying hard not to think about, yet couldn't seem to escape.

"Go write," Sam said.

"Will do. I'll also fax the lists I need you to go over." She rooted around her desk for the list of names, all the people who'd RSVP'd that they'd attend the event and contribute, as well, and the master list of invitees. She'd set up an office in the guest bedroom of the old house she'd bought a few months earlier. The magazine gig, which she'd deemed her transitional career, was freelance and allowed her to work from the comfort of her home.

"Hey, did you go down to the water today?" Sam asked quietly.

There was no judgment in her friend's tone, but Carly still felt her back go up for a moment.

She's only trying to help you.

"No. I didn't get a chance to," she lied. Bitter disappointment surged through her at the fact that she had indeed tried. She'd threaded her toes through the sand at the top of the dunes, stared at the crashing waves a mile or so beyond and had been unable to walk any farther toward them. Breathing the calming ocean air hadn't helped much, either, and she'd admitted defeat and headed back toward the house before she had the chance to panic. When she'd returned to her place, she'd closed the windows in her office so she couldn't hear the ocean.

Maybe buying a house on the beach hadn't been the smartest move after all. It had seemed right when she'd retired, or been forced into retirement, depending on how you looked at it, from professional surfing nearly ten months earlier. She'd sold her surfing school in Hawaii and moved to the Northern Florida Coast, settling near

Daytona, a two-hour drive from Vero Beach, where she'd grown up. At twenty-five, she'd been nearing the end of her career, and the younger, faster women were snapping at her heels. She'd had a good run, and an even greater scare in that last tournament, never mind the accident that capped her career.

"Well, you'll try again tomorrow, then. I know you will."

"Thanks, Sam."

"It's going to get better. Don't put so much pressure on yourself. I know you'll surf again, and then you'll be happy."

Carly wasn't nearly as sure as her friend was, but it was good to know she wasn't alone in the world. "I'll have the fantasy for you in about an hour." She clicked the speaker phone off, wound her long, unruly blond hair up into a messy knot and took a drink of Red Bull for fortification. Then she let her palms run over the smooth oak of the old desk she'd picked up at an antique store last month while she brooded.

It was a gorgeous day outside, all blue skies and perfect swells, and she was unable to come out from behind this desk and catch a hollow.

She'd never admit it to anyone, but when she crashed in her last tournament, she'd been more scared than she'd ever been in her life. She'd been much more hurt, too, since she'd garnered a catalogue of horrific injuries, including a fractured vertebra, a broken femur and a fractured skull. Those were just the biggies, and she'd been lucky to get out of the hospital with only a titanium rod in her thigh as a souvenir. She hadn't needed one in her spine, which most likely would've meant never surfing again.

After ten months of extensive rehab, her thigh and back

still ached occasionally, and even though the PCL muscle in her knee had been surgically repaired, it would never be the same, and neither would she.

She'd been planning to retire after one last circuit of the major tournaments, but she hadn't wanted to go out like that. At the time, her repetitive stress injuries were slowing her down, compounded by the fact that she'd kept up with the big dogs. She'd pushed her fears aside with her competitive nature and ridden in some surfing holes that were not for the squeamish. She'd been pounded and had worn her scars with pride.

At the time she was hospitalized, doctors had told her that leaving the competitive world of surfing behind might be the only chance she'd have of getting on a board again. It would have to be for recreation only. She couldn't imagine not climbing on a board ever again, and so she'd agreed with the medical professionals.

She comforted herself with the fact that she hadn't made that decision based on fear, however, she hadn't realized how deeply the accident had rooted itself into her psyche.

She did realize it now, since she still hadn't been able to get herself onto a board although the doctors had given her the thumbs up. That was a whole different kind of fantasy she needed to fulfill.

She picked up the magazine and flipped to the article on the art of fantasy and seduction by Candy Valentine.

For Carly, fantasizing wasn't the problem.

It wasn't easy to find someone to live up to those dreams. Most of the men she'd met never stayed in one place long enough to even think about a relationship. And a commitment was the last thing on anyone's mind in the happy-go-lucky world of beach bums, who didn't want to grow up. She had to admit, she'd been commitment-shy, too. Until Dan, another professional surfer, cruised into town and swept her away.

The relationship ended in disaster when she'd been hurt. He couldn't handle it, he'd told her, and then added, *besides, now we have nothing in common.* From then on, she'd been reluctant about making promises. Casual flings were fine, but she wasn't wading in deeper in the emotion.

Truth be told, most of the men she dated fell far short of her expectations, both in and out of bed. And now she was supposed to be helping Samantha spice up her reality with a healthy dose of fantasy.

The irony was enough to make her choke on her Red Bull.

She couldn't worry about that now. Fantasize, she ordered herself. She'd use positive visualization, just like her old coach had taught her. Set your sights on your goal and picture yourself attaining it.

She opened a new Word document and began to type quickly, not thinking too hard about the words that flew from her fingers. That was the key to these things, and that's what Candy had written in her latest article:

1. Loosen up, forget the embarrassment.
2. Ask for what you want.
3. Write what thrills you, what turns you on.
4. Explore your deepest sexual secrets.

What was her ultimate fantasy? Beyond getting back up on the board again, of course.

Take the reins and please me.

Really, the line between catching a swell and an orgasm was pretty fine. Both gave that in-the-pit-of-your-belly thrill, and both ended up leaving you wiped out and breathless in the best way possible. The only problem was that surfing was a solitary sport, and she didn't want her orgasms to follow suit.

Let me lose control like I've never lost control before.

She thought about her prince charming, her hero, her everything rolled into one man, and then thought about how, even though she could more than handle herself, she'd like to be handled by him.

Just take me, dammit.

Yep, fantasy was much better than reality.

"YOU NEED A DATE FOR YOUR sister's wedding, Carolyn, and so does Evan. I don't understand the problem."

No, of course her mother wouldn't. Carly bit her tongue. For the millionth time that day, she wished she was still getting her stress-relief from a ride on a wave. Catching a sick double-overhead, especially, and riding through to the crest would've been the perfect remedy for this situation. But she knew she'd been lucky to have avoided her sister's wedding hoopla for this long. The day was imminent now, and it was only a matter of time before her command performance as Carolyn Winters, society maven-to-be.

As if the lime-green bridesmaid's dress wasn't humiliation enough. And she couldn't bear to think about the ridiculous hairstyle she'd have to endure on Nicole's behalf. She'd heard rumors about mini-tiaras, and she hadn't had the heart to investigate it any further.

"Evan's not my type," Carly said.

"But he likes you," her father pointed out.

For *your* money, she thought. For me, all by my lonesome, not so much.

"He's not going to be my date for Nicole's wedding."

It came out louder than intended. Across the table, her father winced and her mother shook her head with impatience, and Carly was glad they'd chosen to eat in at her house, rather than make a public spectacle of themselves.

She'd fallen in love with the old place the second she'd laid eyes on it, despite the real estate agent's pleas to forget about it and find something newer. *Hurricane-proof* was the exact term she'd used. But the small Mediterranean had a charm, a grace one didn't find easily in a house for sale in this part of Florida anymore. The area was rife with McMansions and ranch houses. It had become her safe haven, close enough to the ocean for her to know it was there, but not too close to cause her concern. Until today's fiasco.

"Will you please talk to her?" her mother said to her father while waving a perfectly French-manicured hand in the air.

Everything about her mother was perfect. Shelia Winters was still beautiful, still resembled that young woman who'd won the Miss Florida pageant when she was eighteen and caught the eye of the very wealthy Carl Winters III. Today, her mother's light blue linen suit set off her blue eyes. Her skin seemed untouched by the sun. How someone lived in Florida and managed not to get a tan had always been a mystery to Carly, who only had to think about sun before her skin turned golden brown.

Her mother was already investigating dermabrasion and face lifts for her daughter.

"I'm still in the room," Carly reminded them, dishing herself another helping of the complicated Shrimp Risotto she'd ordered from the gourmet restaurant in town. Cooking had never been her forte, and she'd lived in and out of hotel rooms and rental houses so often that she'd never had the time nor the inclination to learn to cook.

"Honestly, she's impossible." Her mother ran a hand over her own blond hair pulled back in a chic twist.

Carly ran a hand through her mess of blond locks that tumbled loosely around her shoulders. As far from a beauty queen as you could get. Thank goodness her sister had taken on that role willingly, or Carly's teen years would've truly been a nightmare.

"I don't understand the problem, Carolyn," her father said. He was a good match for her mother, still handsome with streaks of silver feathering his dark hair. "You two always enjoyed being together."

"When we were twelve. And it was more of a forced being together, since we were the only two kids of the same age on the yacht," she pointed out.

"We've always talked about the two of you becoming a couple, honey," her mother tried again in her best I'm-trying-to-be-patient-with-you voice. "It seems so right. You're single, he's single…"

Carly sighed, fighting the urge to lie on the floor in the middle of her kitchen and throw a good, old-fashioned temper tantrum. She was a mature, independent and successful woman who happened to be single, but she felt anything but mature right now. Her parents' nagging about dating always seemed to bring out the worst in her, and she'd promised herself their comments wouldn't get to her tonight.

A pairing between Carly and Evan Tremont III was always the family joke, since their parents were best friends. She'd run into Evan maybe three times over the past five years, and none of those events had been memorable. Obviously, both families thought that attending a wedding together might spark some ideas. Evan had no problem with this theory, and no backbone, either, since he'd sent her an e-mail offering to be her date. He'd apologized for being out of the country and unable to ask her in person, but knew they'd have a nice time.

A nice time. Not a great time, an awesome time, a killer-wicked time, not even a good time, but a nice time.

Ultra-formal, ultra-stuffy and ultra-boring. Carly could not live her life like that at all. Evan needed a healthy dose of Candy Valentine and then some.

Evan would've been perfect for Nicole, but her sister always managed to find her own suitably wealthy men their parents approved of. The man she was set to marry in two weeks' time was no exception.

"We're only trying to help, honey. It's been a long time since we've heard about you dating anyone," her mother spoke up.

"I go on dates," Carly insisted. "I didn't realize I had to file a report every time I went out with someone."

She'd had exactly two dates since she'd been back. One was a double date with Samantha and Joe and one of Joe's friends, an experience she'd never repeat. The other was a blind date, the son of someone she knew from the magazine. A total and complete disaster. She'd find her own dates from now on.

"We think you need to start doing something serious with your life, some settling down," her mother continued.

"I was doing something serious. I had a career, remember?"

Her mother rolled her eyes as though she'd sooner forget and her father patted her hand. "Yes, sweetie, but it was time for you to give that up. There's important charity work for you to do in the family's name. People are counting on you."

Inwardly she cringed at the thought of her entire career

being so easily dismissed even though she should be used to it by now. Besides, in surfing, you were only as good as your last ride.

"And I spoke to a plastic surgeon. He said he could remove that with no problem." Her mother pointed to the small tattoo of a shark Carly had on her right ankle as though it were a disease spreading over her daughter's body. "I'm sure he could do something about those, too." This time, her mother pointed to the constant reminders of the accident on Carly's thigh and knee, then waved her hand around, as though making it all disappear.

"I'm not seeing a plastic surgeon. The scars stay. And so does the tattoo." She didn't bother to use the plural. Her mother would never find out about the other one, anyway.

"She's always been so stubborn, Carl." Her mother shook her head and her father sighed.

"Maybe if you gave Evan another chance," her father began. "Nicole doesn't want you dateless at her wedding."

In actuality, she didn't give a flying crap what her perfect younger sister, and former Miss Florida, wanted, but Carly's next words came as much of a surprise to her as they did to her parents. "I'm already seeing someone."

The declaration stopped her parents short and Carly gave herself a mental pat on the back. The technique that had proven successful in several top-grossing movies was obviously as effective in real life.

Time to watch those films again to figure out exactly how these women found their made-up boyfriends.

"You said you were dating, but you didn't mention anyone serious, Carolyn. Why haven't we met this mystery man?" her mother asked.

She'd been thinking the same thing. "He's been away. Traveling. I was going to introduce you at the wedding."

The overactive imagination was good for a lot of things, including making up men in her life. And the traveling excuse came naturally, since she'd done it often for her own career. Why hadn't she thought of this before?

"Why not bring him to the rehearsal dinner?" her mother asked.

Yes. That was why.

"Or, better yet, the party we're throwing this weekend?" her father suggested.

Sure. She'd get right on that magic voodoo doll and conjure herself up a man. At least, her parents had stopped mentioning Evan.

The phone rang, saving her momentarily.

Sam's number flashed on the cell phone's screen. "Hey," Carly whispered, "parents are here." She leaned her back against the cool, white stucco wall in her front hallway.

"Is it as bad as we thought?"

"Worse. Remind me to tell you about the trouble I've created for myself." She heard her parents move into the living room and she made a dash into the now deserted kitchen to start the strong coffee she knew she was going to need.

Sam groaned. "With your imagination, I can only imagine. And I don't mean to bug you, but Joe's coming over tonight and I really wanted to give him that letter."

"It should be easy for you to finish it off. Didn't you like what I wrote?" Carly asked as she crumbled coconut onto the white icing of the cake she'd baked earlier from a box mix. Coconut therapy, she'd joked to herself when she'd made it, and she'd used an extra thick layer of frosting to hide the lopsidedness.

"I'm sure I will, once you send it."

A slight chill went through her at Sam's words. "I sent it hours ago. It went through, because I got the confirmation."

"It didn't come through here," Samantha said quickly. "Can you resend it?"

Resending it was not the most immediate problem. That fax contained some erotic stuff, and whoever got it would most certainly be in for a thrill.

"Sam," Carly said, trying to swallow her panic. "If you didn't get the fax, then who did?"

"Maybe it didn't go through and you only thought it did," Sam tried to reassure her, as she forgot her parents and headed to her office, taking the stairs two at a time.

She pulled the fax confirmation out of the recycling bin where she'd tossed it earlier. She scanned for the number and read it out loud, number by number until…

"I reversed the last two numbers and somehow I added a dash," she said. Oh crap. And then she saw the initials underneath the confirmation. USN. "What the heck does USN stand for?"

"I don't know what it stands for, but I'm sure whoever gets it will just ignore it."

This certainly made finding a man a little less intense, but at least she'd signed Candy's name as a joke and not her own. She hadn't used a cover letter, either.

Whoever got it wasn't going to know it was her personal secret fantasy. "I hope so. And I'll fax it to you again now, okay?" Carly snapped the cell phone shut and double- checked the fax number twice before pushing Send.

"Carolyn, someone's at the door," her mother called up the stairs.

"I've got it," she called back. She crumpled up the confirmation paper and threw it back into the bin before heading down to the front door. She opened it without looking through the peephole.

Camouflage greeted her. A brick wall of camouflage, leaning against her doorjamb with a very serious look on his very good-looking face.

A face she had to look up to see, which, at her own height of five feet, ten inches, meant this man was much taller than that. He was well over six feet and filled out in all the right places.

The army-green T-shirt fit more than fine across his broad chest and shoulders and showed off his sculpted biceps. His dark blond hair was sun-bleached in places, fell across his forehead casually. She was close enough to notice the flecks of gold in his hazel eyes, and a primitive thrill coiled in her belly.

Maybe just thinking about the voodoo doll had worked, because this was more magic than she could've hoped for.

"Can I help you?" she asked.

"Yes, you can." His voice was husky and unhurried as he leaned in toward her, his arm still resting on the doorjamb. "You want to explain why you're sending pornographic faxes to a United States Navy SEAL team?"

2

Hunt hadn't been sure what to expect from someone named Candy Valentine, but the woman who'd answered the door looked genuinely surprised, which was a good sign. It meant the letter had been faxed by mistake, that she wasn't some kind of SEAL groupie or, worse, hadn't been trying to hack the system. In truth, the teams got letters like this one all the time, by mail. But when it came through a secure fax line, it had to be investigated, and he'd been the lucky one pulling office duty at the Mayport Military Base when the fax rolled through the nearest printer.

He was checking in regularly while on partial leave, and he'd never expected to find himself making the hour or so drive down the coast toward Daytona to investigate something like this.

I want you to start by running your tongue slowly around my ear....

Hooyah.

"Who are you?" she asked, keeping her voice low and giving a quick look over her shoulder.

She wasn't home alone. Married, maybe?

"Lieutenant Jonathan Huntington, United States Navy," he announced, letting his gaze drop to her hand. No ring and no tan line. "Did you send this fax?" He held the papers up, page one on top so she could read it.

She licked her bottom lip nervously, and then nodded. Damn, she was sexy.

Let your hand drift down to my breasts….

He'd needed a frozen-cold shower before venturing to find the author. A cursory check through records told him that the owner of the fax line was a woman. He was relieved, but now…

Get down on your knees….

If a fantasy was going to turn him on this much, he sure as hell wanted it to be from someone who looked like her.

A beautiful woman. A woman with tousled blond curls and deep brown eyes and a lithe, athletic-looking body, showcased in a pair of shorts and a tank top.

Spread my thighs….

She had the longest legs he'd ever seen, tanned and slim and finely muscled, and if he wasn't mistaken there was a shark tattoo on her left ankle.

Make me lose control.

You have been OUTCONUS for too long, Hunt—out of the country and out of the bedroom. This was a hell of a welcome home. It was time for some much needed R & R, and he wondered what this Candy Valentine was up to.

A list of names had been faxed along with the fantasy, some of which read like a who's who of Florida society. He'd grown up in the area, close enough to know the wealthy by name but not close enough for any of it to rub off on him. And there was an expensive, top-of-the-line Mercedes convertible in her driveway.

Was it possible she was some kind of high-priced call girl?

"This is an extremely serious offense." He continued to play the hard ass, although now his curiosity was more than piqued. Especially because of the thin, healing scars running vertically along her right thigh and knee. "The military doesn't look kindly on solicitations of this kind."

But this letter sure as hell does it for me.

"It…this…wasn't supposed to be," she stuttered, and then she stopped and gained her composure. "I'm sorry about the mistake. This was supposed to go to a friend and I obviously faxed it to the wrong number. I apologize for the inconvenience."

"A male friend?"

"Excuse me?"

"You said it was supposed to go to a friend…."

"Oh. No. It was for a female friend." Her blush was visible through her tan, and she shifted from one bare foot to the other as she crossed her arms. "It's not what you think."

"I'm thinking a lot of things right now," he said.

"I don't see how the specifics are any of your business. I'll take those back and you can be on your way." She reached out for the papers but he pulled them away.

"No can do. It's official government property."

"What does the government want with something like that?"

"It's become part of our records. Any and all unauthorized documents that come through our fax lines have to be investigated and properly recorded." That wasn't exactly true. It was also up to his discretion as to whether or not to drop this matter, but watching her defend herself was turning him on almost as much as her words on paper had.

"So there's going to be a file somewhere in our federal government titled Carly's Fantasy?" she demanded.

Hell yes, only it's going to be in my personal file.

"I don't know who Carly is," he spoke with a formal tone. "This fax was sent by Candy Valentine."

Busted. Her mouth dropped for a second, but again, he gave her credit for her quick pick-up. "Carly's my nickname," she offered, and then looked angry at herself for giving him that information. The nickname fit her—she looked like a Carly. She looked really, really good, too, and he wondered if it would be against any and all regulations to ask her out on a date, right then and there.

After he did his job and got this mess sorted out, of course. After he found out that she wasn't a hooker.

"I'd appreciate it if you could tell me how you got ahold of a secure fax number. And why you're using an alias."

"It was a mistake. I reversed the last two numbers and I'm not using an alias. And *I'd* appreciate it if we could let the whole matter go." She was telling the truth on both counts. He could tell by the way her gaze held his steadily and the way she kept her voice low, so whoever was in the next room couldn't overhear.

She was a woman with a secret, but she'd already spilled some pretty personal ones on the papers he held in his hand.

"You look familiar," he said suddenly, and that wasn't just a pick-up line. "I've seen you somewhere before…."

"Well, you haven't. So if you'll give me back those pages, I won't tell anyone about this."

He could do that. Or he could take this whole thing one step further and risk having her call his superiors.

He was used to tougher risks than this. "So tell me, Carly. Is *this* one of your fantasies?"

The flush spread again, over her nose and the smattering of freckles. "Are you here to make fun of me or to find out if I'm some kind of terrorist fantasy-writer?"

"I'm not here to make fun of you," he said.

"Then what are you going to do about this? Are you letting it drop?"

"There are two problems I have to deal with before I can do that."

"And what would those be?"

"First of all, I need to know how and why you have a list like this, complete with addresses and phone numbers of some of the wealthiest people in Palm Beach."

"And what's the second problem?"

He leaned in and smiled. "You didn't finish the fantasy."

"Carolyn? What's going on?" An attractive woman, who looked much younger than she probably was, came up behind Carly and smiled when she saw him. "Oh, I'm sorry, dear. I didn't realize you had company. Aren't you going to introduce us to your friend?"

THE CHANCES OF A situation like this happening were slim to none.

The chance of you taking that wave is slim to none, Carly, her old coach's voice echoed in her ear. On that particular day, the odds had been in her favor. The trophy was situated proudly in her office.

It seemed as if her life was full of chances the bookmakers wouldn't dare gamble on. So what was one more?

Oh, this was so *not* good.

"Mother," she began, well aware this man could probably read the slight panic that had to be showing on her face.

Said man stepped forward and extended a hand. "Pleased to meet you. I'm Jonathan Huntington, but you can call me Hunt."

"Hello, Hunt." Carly would've laughed at the way her

mother said the nickname, but she was beyond having fun. "I'm Carolyn's mother, Sheila Winters."

Her father came from nowhere and shook Hunt's hand. "Carl Winters III. You must be related to the West Palm Huntingtons."

"No, sir."

"Ah, the New York Huntingtons then. Huntington Oil."

Again, Hunt shook his head. "I grew up a short distance from here, but my family wasn't in the oil business."

This was like living in some alternative universe where things like erotic faxes and sailors and parents ended up together in one place. This was not the planet Earth Carly knew and loved.

"And you're in the military?" her mother asked, and Carly gave her mental kudos for changing the subject so deftly. Part of the whole white-glove upbringing.

"Yes, ma'am."

"Well, we're very patriotic. In fact, I ran a charity auction for our troops last month."

"We appreciate the support," he said.

"So, this is the gentleman you were telling us about, Carolyn?" her mother asked.

Just kill me now.

Heck, for all she knew, Hunt could be an axe murderer.

"Um," she said, looking into Hunt's eyes and wondering how far he would be willing to go with this ruse. He hadn't mentioned the fax yet, so maybe she could get through this with some pride intact.

"I guess that's why my ears were burning. I just got off work and stopped by to see if Carly wanted to catch some dinner," he said without a trace of hesitation in his voice. He grabbed her hand, his thumb traced her palm and then he brought it to his mouth and kissed it.

Okay. Not an axe murderer, but he was definitely going to kill her if he kept doing things like that.

Samantha was right. It had been way too long for Carly. And she wanted a lot more than dinner. She wanted to sink into the sand, never to be seen again. Then again, a big part of her wouldn't mind pulling Hunt down with her.

He knew her fantasy, knew how she wanted to be touched and where....

No, he didn't know anything, she told herself firmly. When her parents left, she'd explain things to this Hunt person. He was in the military, and they must have a code, or some kind of moral obligation that would make him keep his mouth shut and protect her secret.

Why else was he playing along with this dinner thing?

"We've finished dinner, but we haven't had dessert yet. Why don't you join us?" Sheila Winters asked.

"Dessert sounds great," Hunt said with obvious enthusiasm. Carly fought a gasp and squeezed his hand instead, since he hadn't released hers. He took the opportunity to pull her closer and she swore he was hypnotizing her parents, right in front of her.

Granted, it was a trick she'd be more than happy to learn.

"I'll pour the coffee. Come help me, Carl," her mother urged with a smile on her face. A smile. Hunt definitely had to have some kind of special superpowers, which didn't bode well for her.

When her parents were a safe distance away, she whispered, "What do you think you're doing?"

"Apparently, helping you out of a jam," he said with an innocent shrug. It would have worked, too, except the man was far from innocent. There was something so commanding about his presence that she'd been ready to spill everything, until common sense had taken over.

Hunt was in the military, and all the guys probably gave off that air. Still, she'd known him for less than five minutes and she already knew he was nothing like any man she'd ever met. What were the chances…

"Wait a minute. I thought SEALs were stationed in California and Virginia?"

"We pop up in a lot of unexpected places," he said.

"I'll bet you do. And how will you pull this off?" she asked.

"How will *we* pull this off, is the bigger question? Because your parents think I'm your significant other, and you didn't tell them I'm not."

"You went along with it."

"You seemed a little desperate."

"Why are you doing this?" Why wasn't he letting go of her hand?

"I want to know what happens at the end."

He obviously wasn't aware that the fantasy was always better than the reality. The problem was that the two had, moments ago, collided head-on, and she was caught inside the wave, while he'd aced her with a total 360, leaving her nowhere to bail.

In a surfer's world that signaled a potential wipe-out. It was definitely time to kick out of this man's wave. "You go home, and I have to tell my parents you're not my boyfriend." She took her hand back from his and immediately missed the contact.

"I'm nobody's boyfriend, Carly. But I wasn't talking about after dessert. I was talking about the end of this fantasy." Hunt smiled a wide, wicked grin and winked, then he sauntered past her into the house. "I hope you made my favorite, honey," he said loudly. "Because I'm in the mood for some sugar."

3

SUGAR HAD BEEN THE first thing on his mind, too. Maybe that could finally put some of the pieces of this puzzle together.

Maybe he could get Carly to reveal more of her fantasy, although he'd finished it off a dozen different ways in his mind already.

It had been a long drive, and the steady hum of the bike vibrating between his legs made the highway one long pre-orgasmic stretch.

Now, he forced himself to tamp down the enthusiastic buzz as he sat across the table from Sheila and Carl Winters. He'd recognized their names immediately when he'd seen them on the list. They were upper high society in the small Vero Beach community, always making the papers for one thing or another.

Carly Winters was one interesting lady even without the fax. And, from the strained look on her face, he had to guess that the erotic fax thing wouldn't go over well with this set.

How he'd suddenly become the long-lost boyfriend was anybody's guess.

"So Hunt, are you a Marine?"

He fought the urge to yell, *hell no,* and instead said calmly, "No, ma'am. I'm a Navy SEAL."

"Would you mind my asking what a SEAL is?"

He smiled at Sheila Winters, because at least that answer was easy. "We're part of the Special Operations division. SEAL is an acronym for sea, air and land. Although we're primarily known for our water ability we can pretty much handle any assignment, regardless of the terrain. We're Navy and we work in small teams."

"So you've probably traveled all over the world."

To crapholes you haven't even dreamed of visiting. "Yes, ma'am, although I can't say much more than that. All of our missions are classified."

"Well, is how you and Carly met classified information?" Sheila asked him, a tiny smile on her face. From behind her parents, Carly smirked at him as she brought the coconut cake to the table in the center of the large kitchen.

He raised his eyebrows and she jumped in hurriedly. "At the beach. We met at the beach."

Safe enough answer. Safer than the truth, and he could work with it.

"Was it at one of her competitions?" Carl Winters asked.

"Oh, Carl, please. Do we have to discuss that? I'm so happy she's not doing that surfing thing anymore. I was always so worried about her."

He'd seen two longboards propped up outside the house. And suddenly, he remembered where he'd seen Carly Winters. The local paper had run a lengthy article on her a few months back when he'd been in town for training and when she'd retired her pro-surfing status.

Wow. "Unfortunately, I didn't get to see her in action," he said, watching the blush spread across her cheeks again. He could think of a lot better ways to make her blush.

"She had a good career," Carl said. "I have some old tapes I could lend you that show her competing."

"That'd be great. From what I hear, she was amazing to watch."

Carly threw him a strange look, somewhere between appreciation and pain. He pictured her in a bikini, riding the hell out of a wave along the swells of the ocean. Had to be a thing of beauty.

A SEAL and a surfer. There were worse combinations, and this particular one could prove to be a hell of a ride.

"She was a wonderful surfer," Carl agreed.

Sheila changed the subject with a wave of her hand to her husband. "So, how long have you two been seeing each other?"

"Six months," Hunt answered, figuring a nice, even number was the way to go. Besides, if he'd guessed wrong, it would be okay. Guys were supposed to screw up stuff like anniversaries and birthdays.

"So you met before she moved back here, then."

Ah, screwed that one up. Still, he nodded, mind firmly set in interrogation mode. They didn't need to know he wasn't permanently stationed around here.

"Yes. He was training in Hawaii," Carly said. And that made sense. Surfing. Hawaii.

"And you've been traveling, Carolyn tells us," Sheila Winters continued.

Sounds about right.... "Yes. I've been overseas, so I'm looking forward to spending more time with Carly." Where was this stuff coming from? Maybe he had an acting career after his SEAL stint?

"And he's back just in time for the wedding," Carly added.

Whoa. Wedding? Hell, he'd do anything for his

country, and obviously a lot to help out and help himself to a beautiful stranger, but no how, no way was he getting roped into marriage. Suddenly, the kitchen shrank to the size of a cell and a strong survival urge kicked in. He was telling himself to get out, hit the open road and rock on.

Although the thought of tossing the surfer over his shoulder, before giving her parents the peace out, didn't seem too bad.

THE WEDDING QUESTION HAD stopped him cold. Nice to know the thought of commitment could bring even a tough-guy, Navy SEAL to his knees.

Carly should've let him choke, but she needed him. This had gone too far, and she didn't want to look like a bigger fool than she already was. "You remember, I told you my sister's getting married, right?" She gave him a look with a raise of her eyebrows as she slid the plate in front of him. "The wedding's in two weeks."

"Right. I must've forgotten," he said, and took a bite of the cake.

"I'm sure you had many other things on your mind while you were away." Her mother took a demure sip of coffee and pushed her cake away after only a cursory bite.

This *was* a way for Carly to get her parents off her back. She could show up at the wedding alone, claim a last minute breakup. By then, it would be too late to pair her with Evan, and hopefully, he'd have his own date.

"There's a party we're throwing next week, and then there's the rehearsal dinner, too. I need to tell the chef if we're expecting another person, you understand," her mother explained.

This wasn't happening. There wasn't enough coconut therapy in the world to help Carly now.

"Yes, I do." Hunt finished his piece of cake and slung an arm around her shoulders. His closeness was comforting, like a protective shield. "I'm actually on partial duty for the next month, so my schedule's pretty light."

And it was getting worse by the second, like a complete train wreck she couldn't do a thing to stop. Like it was happening in somebody else's life, not hers, and she'd wake up to find out this was all a strange dream. A strange dream that included a dark blond, green-eyed, handsome man, who made her toes curl every time she looked at him.

She crossed her arms in front of her and he looked at her as if he could read her mind.

Then again, he didn't need to. She'd written it all out on paper.

"So you're coming to the wedding, then?" her mother repeated.

"Wouldn't miss it. I don't like disappointing Carly," Hunt said, giving her shoulder a squeeze.

She could imagine what was going through her mother's mind right now. Organizing a charity event for the military was one thing, but having her eldest daughter bring a Navy SEAL to a family wedding was quite another, especially when said daughter was supposed to have her hand spoken for.

It almost made up for the fact that later on, Carly would have to explain this whole thing to Hunt. She was going to owe him big-time, and she had a sneaking suspicion about what he'd want for payment.

"Sheila, we should go and leave these kids alone. I'm sure they don't want us hanging around." Her father stood to leave and Hunt stood as well.

"Please don't leave on my account."

"We've got a drive ahead of us back to Vero," her

mother said. "We'll see you both on the sixteenth for the party."

They'd see *her* there, but she and Hunt would be long broken up by then, because this was a big mistake. Or maybe they'd be visiting her in a military prison reserved for erotic-fantasy writers. Either way, she was screwed.

She walked her parents to the door.

"Dinner was lovely, Carolyn. And Hunt seems like a very nice young man." Her mother gave her a quick peck on the cheek and Carly wondered if Hunt had ever been called a very nice young man. "You will have to let Evan know about your change of plans. Perhaps he'll realize he's got to work a little harder to get through to you."

Useless to argue. Obviously, Hunt's powers of mind control only worked during direct contact. "I'll talk to Evan. And I'll see you guys next week." Carly gave a quick wave as they got into their car and backed out of the driveway.

When she returned she found Hunt comfortably en-sconced on her sofa, flipping through a surfing magazine. He'd kicked off his flip-flops, which didn't look as if they belonged to any official Navy uniform, and his cell phone and beeper were strewn on her coffee table. He'd also cut himself a second piece of coconut cake and poured another cup of coffee. He appeared to be camping out for a while.

Meaning it was time for her to decide how far to take this situation. "Look, I don't know why you did what you did—"

"Think they bought it?" he interrupted, and she found herself staring at him again. He was so handsome. Quickly, a dozen different fantasies, all involving Hunt and his uniform and a nice hot game of "Yes, ma'am" seemed like a great way to pass the night.

But it was a fantasy that had gotten her into this particular mess to start with. "Yes, they did buy it. Now, I'll have to think up some excuse as to why you won't be attending any Winters family functions. What were you thinking?"

"You started it. You were the one who sent me the fantasy."

"I didn't send *you* any fantasy. I told you, it was a mistake." A giant, horrifically embarrassing mistake.

"I like a woman who knows what she wants." His voice dropped an octave as his gaze swept over her. "And you don't have anything to be embarrassed about."

"Are you going to turn that document in?"

"No, I'm not," he replied, and she breathed a sigh of relief as he handed it to her, along with the guest lists.

"Well, thanks. And thanks for trying to help tonight. I didn't mean to pull you into this."

"Looks like you owe me," he told her, watching her with that I've-got-plans-for-you gaze.

"The cake wasn't enough?"

"Not nearly enough." He'd abandoned the coffee as he stood, stretched and stared at her appreciatively. On any other guy, it would've been obscene. On him, it made her want to take off her clothes. Or better yet, let him take them off. Slowly.

"We just met, Hunt. I don't even know you," she said, as more of a reminder to herself than anything.

"I'm an open book," he said, shrugging his shoulders, and Carly thought about asking him to reveal one of his fantasies, so that they'd be on a level playing field. "It's not like we had a date or anything," she continued, realizing he didn't need any more ammunition than what he already had on her. He didn't seem the type who'd have any problem spilling his fantasies. Fantasies involving his removing that T-shirt and letting her check out what she was sure was the best chest she'd ever seen, which probably had a light dusting of blond hair leading down to his...

"You don't seem like a woman who'd get caught up in conventions. And I am invited to the wedding." He grinned, and she wondered if this man could indeed read minds.

Carly narrowed her eyes. "And what's in this for you?"

"I already told you. I want to know how the fantasy ends." Hunt moved closer, and she wanted to walk away, to tell him to go right out her front door and not come back, but she couldn't. Her feet remained rooted in place as he stood inches from her, and tension crackled the air between them.

What was in that coconut cake? Aphrodisiac therapy. Coconut covered SEAL.

She needed to get a grip.

But the memory of what she'd written was almost too much to bear, and the thought of putting it to practice, and putting Hunt to the test, was making her hot.

His scent reminded her of the beach in the early morning, so full of promise, hinting of sunshine and ideal waves. It was her favorite smell and a longing echoed inside of her. It would be so easy to kiss him, to make her fantasy come true. There was nothing stopping her from stripping off her clothes and having Hunt press his body against hers, letting him take her against the couch, or on the floor, or anywhere else he wanted to.

It would be the easiest thing.

He remained close to her, his lips parted in a seductive smile before he spoke. "Are you going to tell me how it ends? Or do you want me to show you first how I'd finish it?"

4

HE DIDN'T WAIT TO HEAR her answer before he brought his mouth down on hers. It was a slow, warm kiss that threatened to turn into something molten. Hunt's hands were in her hair. Carly's hands were fisted against his chest, unsure if they were there to pull him closer or push him away.

She had an open invitation to show him how she'd end it, any way she wanted. Who could pass that up?

Choosing the road less taken, Carly knew she'd regret it one way or another. She pulled back, breaking the kiss without finesse.

His smile was wider than it had been before. His green eyes slightly more golden, and his thick blond hair begged for her to thread her hands in it. She knew taking him to bed was the only right thing to do. "I think you need to leave, Hunt," she said.

"I don't think you mean that."

Of course she didn't, but it had taken every ounce of strength to stop and still have a coherent thought. He tasted like coconut. He tasted delicious and he kissed her the way someone who knew how to kiss should. He should teach courses in kissing, because that's how good it was. Over the falls paled in comparison.

She didn't need any more distractions.

He stepped back and released her, but made no move to leave. "So tell me again why a professional surfer girl is faxing erotic fantasies to strangers."

"Former pro surfer girl," she corrected. "And I told you. I was helping out a friend."

"Right, a friend. So where did this idea for the fax come from, anyway?"

She thought for a second about not telling him, and then figured he might as well know the whole truth rather than continue thinking she was plain crazy.

Carly dug out the magazine from the pile next to her couch and handed it to him. He read for a minute in silence and she got a chance to stare at him a little more. Because there was something about this man in uniform that made her tingle.

"So you needed to spice up your sex life?" he asked finally.

"I told you, it wasn't for me. My friend needed to spice up hers. I was giving her a start with the fantasy."

"And how did things work out for your friend?"

"I'll find out in the morning," she said, smiling.

"Candy Valentine's a good name, but it sounds like a stripper. Is that part of your fantasy?"

"I'm sure it's part of yours."

"Oh, yeah. That would work." He eyed the matching decorative columns that ran, floor to ceiling, in her living room.

Oh boy.

"These are really cool," he said. He'd moved into an alcove, scanning the pictures she'd hung there. Most of them were photos of her having just come off a ride, and a few boasted her on the covers of some surfing magazines, one of them a national publication. She'd debated not hanging them up at all, but hoped having that daily public reminder would inspire her to get better. Fixed. Something.

Seeing a therapist was the next step. She didn't want it to have to come to that. Admitting the problem had been hard enough.

Admitting the problem to her parents was something she didn't plan on doing, period. And really, she could easily back out of her mother's upcoming charity event by citing pain. There were plenty of other surfers and body boarders participating. Some recognizable names were giving their time to raise money for spinal cord injury research. But she'd booked herself as one of the attractions because her pride wouldn't let her do otherwise. She still held out more than a spark of hope that she could give an impromptu, two-minute ride on a longboard, and influence some girl the way she'd been influenced so many years ago. And now, two weeks and counting, she couldn't make it mid-beach, never mind into the water. She had her strength back, and enough flexibility to let her give a decent ride.

"Where'd you learn to surf?" Hunt asked, pulling her from her reverie. She realized she been fisting her hands so tightly that her nails had left marks in her palms. She straightened her hands and rubbed them against each other as she spoke.

"I grew up hanging around on the beach," she replied. "It was the thing to do."

A charity event her mother dragged her to. She remembered being hot and itchy in the stupid dress she'd been forced into. Aged ten, and already more trouble than her parents cared to handle. She'd wandered off after the event, which was some kind of Save Our Oceans campaign, and she'd happened upon a woman who stood by the water's edge carrying a surfboard.

All the surfers Carly had seen in her life up till that point had been men, and she'd been curious. The woman took off in the water, paddled out and caught a ride. It left Carly fascinated. The next day, she'd begged her dad for surfing lessons and he'd agreed.

"And you made a career out of it," Hunt said.

"I did. Pretty cool to make a living doing something you love." She couldn't help but smile as she remembered how awesome it was.

"So what are you going to do now that you've retired? It has to be something that lets you get your kicks because I can't imagine you driving a desk." Instead of thinking about his words, she wanted to rub her cheek against the slight rough on his face and let it tickle her. "More dessert?" she asked. She didn't wait for his response before grabbing his plate and heading for the kitchen.

CARLY RETURNED A FEW minutes later with what looked like half the cake. He'd stretched out on her couch again, planned on getting, and staying, comfortable, then smiled as he took the plate from her. "Thanks."

"Sure."

"So, we were talking about what you're planning now, career-wise." he said.

"Right. Well, what are you going to do when you leave the SEALs?" she asked finally, and he caught more than a hint of defensiveness in her tone.

Yeah, it was more than a touchy subject for her.

Her body posture changed, tensed up, almost the way it had when her parents mentioned her career. Too many people had asked her that question and she didn't have a sure-fire answer yet. He was almost sorry he'd brought it up. But he lived by instinct and something told him there was more to her retirement than met the eye, scars or no scars. Every professional athlete had their share of those, and he wondered if they had anything to do with her bowing out early.

"Hadn't thought about it much, since I don't have plans to leave the military anytime soon."

"I didn't have plans, either," she said quietly. Too quietly.

"Sometimes plans aren't always the answer."

She nodded and then seemed to realize she'd given away more than she'd wanted to. "This has been an interesting night, but—"

"But it's not over yet," he said. "Let's take a walk on the beach. It's a perfect way to end our date."

She hesitated long enough for him to know something wasn't right. It had nothing to do with her wanting him out of there. She didn't want him gone; her body was giving off all the wrong signals.

He knew when a body turned traitor, and besides that, Carly Winters didn't have a poker face. And she hadn't even bitten on the date comment.

"I'm kind of tired," she said.

"It's only eight o'clock."

"I've got an early day ahead of me."

"More faxing?"

She rolled her eyes at him. "Fine. A quick walk." She slid the glass door open and they stepped out onto her portico and headed to the dunes just beyond.

All the stars were out. A beautiful, calm evening, a sight he always looked for when he was on a mission and one he rarely got. He stopped and stared up, drew in a deep breath of sea air before continuing on.

Carly had walked ahead of him, and he watched her outline, silhouetted in the moonlight. She moved easily, with the grace of someone who had a natural athletic ability, and he wondered if he'd get the chance to see her surf anytime soon. Or naked. With or without the surfboard.

Now *that* would be a fantasy come true.

"Are you coming?" she asked.

He bit his tongue and caught up to her with a few easy strides. They walked in silence for several seconds, until they hit the dunes. He jumped over into the soft sand that led to the surf, where high tide had crested, but she remained behind.

"I'm going back," she told him.

"We just got here. And it looks like the night for a swim."

"I'm not wearing my bathing suit." She crossed her arms in front of her and looked anything but comfortable.

"Don't tell me you've never skinny-dipped."

"I'll leave that one to your imagination," she said. "And now you're staring."

"Not staring—imagining."

That got a slight smile from her and yeah, he liked that smile.

"Have you gotten your fill yet?" she asked, even as his eyes lingered on her legs and continued upward, traveling slowly until his gaze met hers.

"Not by a long shot."

"Hunt, look…"

"I'm going in," he called out before she could start talking about heading for the house again. He threw his T-shirt toward her and quickly shed his pants. Modesty in the military wasn't possible, and getting naked was something he'd never been much shy about anyway. "Watch my back."

He broke into a swift run as he got closer to the edge

of the surf, and once his feet hit the water he moved faster until he could dive into the dark waves and roll with the undertow. Night swimming had always been his favorite, even as a kid growing up along the beach. The sound of the rushing water wasn't drowned out by a noisy, touristy beach crowd, and the thrill of doing something he wasn't supposed to only added to the pleasure.

Funny, he'd have bet money a surfer would feel the same way, but Carly was no closer to joining him than she was at the start. If anything, it looked as though she'd backed away from the dunes, but she was still watching him.

Yes, there was a lot more he wanted to find out about that.

5

_____

CARLY WANTED NOTHING more than to strip and run into those dark waves with him. Her muscles ached for it, but her mind wouldn't give in. Before the accident ten months ago, she wouldn't have given his offer a second thought, probably would've been the one suggesting the skinny-dip.

She was no fun anymore.

And when she lost sight of Hunt for a second after a crashing wave broke over him, she held her breath until he resurfaced.

Damn. She hated this, hated herself for being so scared. She held on to Hunt's T-shirt in one hand, picked up his pants with the other and shook the sand from them while he frolicked in the water. There was no underwear to be found, and she guessed the term going commando was indeed coined by the military for a reason.

How did she get involved in all of this?

Right, the movie thing. The I'm-dating-someone-already excuse. The Candy Valentine fantasy.

She _would_ have a lot more fun if she brought along Hunt. The parties she was expected to attend would be boring and stuffy and Hunt could do his magic hypnotizing act on the whole lot of them. He'd probably be a big hit, but had he actually agreed to help her?

He ran back up the sand and stopped in front of her. Salt water dripped off his body which, even with only the moonlight to see by, looked better than anything she'd ever seen in a gym or on a surfer.

Her hands fisted at her sides, nails biting palms again until he let a lazy half smile tug at his mouth. He was standing so close, so naked, daring her to do something, anything. She thought about the way he'd swum out, how powerful his body looked cutting through the moonlit waves.

She wanted some of that power for her own, needed to release the tension that was making her body ache. And her fantasy was standing right there.

She reached out, touched his shoulder, wanting to feel the water on her before it possibly brought on another panic attack. But somehow the combination of Hunt and the sea wasn't scary, at least not with his broad shoulders blocking her view of the waves.

Not scary at all, especially when she used some positive visualization. And at that moment, she was pretty positive about what she wanted.

She leaned into him, and his hands went around her waist, pulled her against him, and she tasted the salt water on his lips, lost herself in his mouth. Her hands tugged at his wet hair while her body molded to his. She wondered why she'd protested earlier. The kiss was warm and tender and she almost forgot to breathe.

She didn't plan on stopping anything, wanted him to put his hands on her, all over her, to make her forget surfing and the wedding and everything except his touch.

As if he understood, his hands went under her tank top. He caressed her back, then drifted leisurely over the curve of her breasts as if he had all the time in the world.

So strong and so right. Her nipple swelled against his palm.

"I bet this is how you like it, Carly," he whispered, running his tongue along the sensitive, outer rim of her ear, leaving a trail of salt water along her shoulder. Hunt captured her lobe in his teeth, nipping while he brushed a thumb over one nipple and then the other with just enough pressure to make her press into it. "You want more, don't you?"

"Yes," she murmured, knowing he'd managed to hypnotize her, too. Knowing she wanted his mouth on her breasts and anywhere else he deemed to kiss her.

He pushed her back and put his mouth over one nipple, which was still covered in the lacy fabric of her bra. He flicked the bud with his tongue. Her breath quickened, and she longed for his tongue rasping her nipple without the barrier.

Impatiently, she pushed him back, tugged her tank top over her head, and he was on her again, unhooking her bra and working a nipple with his tongue.

The strength of his arm around her waist was the only thing holding her up. He was so close, and still, she wanted him closer.

"Hunt, yes," she moaned as he worked the bud in tandem with the hand he'd slid down her shorts. When his fingers slid inside her thong and touched her, she jumped. He chuckled against her breast, worked a finger into her center.

She was ready, so ready for him, and moved against the beat of his hand while he used his arm to steady her. His wasn't letting her nipple go, continued to tug it gently between his teeth, roll it and lick it until she was sure the neighbors would hear her cries above the pounding surf. The need that burned her belly began to tighten—when need met want and urgency couldn't be contained anymore.

"Let go, baby," he whispered against her breast before putting his tongue back to work. She buried her face into his neck, held his shoulders for dear life as the orgasm rocked through her, pulsated against his hand.

When she opened her eyes, she found him watching her, until he slid down on his knees in front of her.

Just like the fantasy.

Hunt pushed her thighs apart, then held her hips and brought his face to her belly. He ran his tongue over her skin, making her shiver. And then he looked up. With that lazy half smile he jolted her already-on-edge nerve endings. Her breath went taut.

And then he got to his feet as disappointment washed over her from head to toe.

"We'd better put some clothes on before your neighbors decide to take a nightly stroll of their own," he suggested.

What had she been thinking? This part of the beach behind her house was secluded, yes, but not private, and several other houses dotted the shoreline and shared the same patch of sand. Anyone could've walked by. Granted, she and Hunt had been more than hidden behind the dune and the tall sea grass, but she was half naked and he was much, much more than that.

"What about you?" she asked, and watched as he pulled his pants on after he'd helped her with her tank top. She stuffed her bra in the pocket of her shorts.

"I'll live," he said. "Besides, it wasn't my fantasy, although it was pretty close."

They walked back toward Carly's house. He caught her hand in his, leading her to the portico and the sliding glass door. She was sure he was going to invite himself in. Better yet, he'd pick her up and carry her inside, up the stairs and into her bedroom.

Hunt's eyes met hers and he smiled. He kissed her again before he sauntered off around the side of her house. After a minute's pause, she heard the engine of the bike—a sound that rumbled through her the way he had, and then it shot away into the distance. No man had that kind of self control.

Obviously, Hunt had, that and a lot more self-restraint than the average man. From what she'd seen, there was nothing about him that could be deemed average.

She wasn't sure if she would see him again, but at least he'd gotten her over the dunes. Literally.

Somehow, even though he had control of the fantasy, she had a sinking feeling the ball had been left in her court. It was sink or swim time for Carly, and she couldn't even get in the water.

She wandered along to the kitchen, a strange combination of utter relief and pent-up energy flowing through her. She thought about calling Sam, and even as her hand reached for the receiver, she remembered that her friend was supposed to be living out her own adventure tonight.

They'd certainly have a lot to discuss, come morning.

6

SAMANTHA GRAYSON WAS going to hunt Candy Valentine down and hurt her. That was the only thing she could think of at first, when Joe uttered those fateful words no woman ever wanted to hear.

"What do you mean, *how can I bring you home to my mother now?*" Sam thought of a few more choice words too, said them, and understood that her last shot of meeting Joe's mother was over. She just wanted Joe out of her apartment, and out of her life. The sooner, the better.

She grabbed her robe and quickly pulled it on over the lacey bra-and-panty ensemble she'd purchased earlier that day. Her plan had been to spice up this relationship even if she died of embarrassment doing so.

She didn't think things could go this downhill this fast. But her boyfriend of four months stood there holding the sexy fantasy in his hand, looking between her and the paper as though both of them scared him.

And here she thought she was the prude.

Joe stared at the paper, and when he spoke, his voice reflected his level of disbelief. "You want to do a striptease for me? You want me to tell you how hot I get when I see you naked? I mean, Samantha, what were you thinking? This is so unlike you."

"I sure wasn't thinking about your mother when I wrote it," she shot back.

"Where did you learn these things? I can't believe you wrote this," he said.

She had written it, the whole thing, from scratch. When Carly's fax finally came through, she'd crumpled it up, threw it away and wrote out her own fantasy. She'd never expected this would be Joe's reaction.

"I was trying to turn you on. I'm sorry you disapprove." What a jerk. He had to be the only man on earth who'd still be standing there, fully clothed and horrified by sexy words. She should've known this was a bad idea from the start, especially since she normally didn't date men who had blood-lines like Joe's. His family was prim and proper, the kind of family who was friendly with Carly's. Joe was the kind of man who shouldn't be with someone who wasn't a debutante. But Sam had always presented as if she belonged in that set, and when Joe set his sights on her, she'd been flattered.

That his kisses left her cold was a fact she'd blamed on herself, until this happened. She was an idiot for forcing her love life into the wrong-shaped box. Because, at the heart of the matter, a man like Joe would never, ever get her blood pumping.

At first, there had been something. Shared interests. A love of Shakespeare and foreign films. And he was handsome. Kind and gentle.

That was the problem. Gentle. Didn't need it or want it. His "I want my girlfriend to be plain vanilla and have sex in the missionary position only," attitude wasn't for her. And partially, it was her fault, since she had yet to allow a man to see past the good girl disguise she wore so well. She'd always imagined that the right man would see through her act, although a big part of her was worried about what would happen when that did happen. Her mother had been a, quote unquote, bad girl, and that hadn't worked out for her at all.

And Joe was still reading, when he should've been ripping her clothes off. "Tie me to the bed…I want to be helpless when you take me…."

"Just stop." She snatched the fantasy from his hands before she did shrivel up and die from humiliation.

"I don't understand. It's like something out of a porno movie." He was hanging on to the paper, but held it away from his body, as if whatever she wrote there was highly contagious.

If only.

"I'm surprised you'd know," she said.

"I do know, but it's not something I want to associate with the woman I'm dating," he spat. "This is something I'd expect from a woman who performs at bachelor parties or strip clubs."

"I thought you'd be happy. I thought it would get you going." Somehow, she'd treaded too closely to Joe's ego, taken away his pride when she'd taken the lead. But if he'd had any kind of mojo in the first place, she wouldn't have had to write the fantasy.

"I think we need to see other people. I thought you were different, and I don't know if we're meant to be together," he said.

"Breaking up's fine with me. I'll buy a vibrator to replace you. It'll fulfill my fantasies better than you ever could. And maybe I'll even send one to your mother."

He stormed out of her apartment, and her tears rose, more from embarrassment and anger than hurt. Though she mentally congratulated herself for being honest about what she wanted in bed. Maybe Candy Valentine was rubbing off on her and didn't deserve to be strangled, after all. Maybe there was something to be said for letting your wild side hang out, because her blood was pumping like it never had before.

Who are you kidding? Come morning, Sam'd be back to her old, safe life. Still, she couldn't bring herself to throw out the written fantasy. Maybe if she slept with it under her pillow, she'd conjure up dreams of a man willing to satisfy her in whatever ways she wanted.

"IS THIS WHAT YOU DO NOW when you get time off? Sit on your ass like an old man, reading the paper? You should be out, raising hell and partying with naughty women. And bringing some along for me."

Ty Huntington's voice carried, loud and raucous, across the quiet diner. His black leather boots were noisy, stomping across the linoleum. In fact, Ty was pretty much dressed totally in black. When he stripped off his jacket it revealed a T-shirt with no sleeves and multiple tattoos adorning both arms.

It was only a little past two in the morning, but Hunt had never slept much anyway. He'd stretched out in one of the back booths to catch up on the news. He'd known his brother would be arriving at some point soon; this diner was always his first stop when he was in town. And Hunt had been right, because he'd heard the roar of Ty's Harley long before his brother pulled into the parking lot. Ty always rigged his bikes to roar so loud when started that they would set off car alarms within four blocks. Luckily, he was always gone before the irate owners got to him.

"I wore all those women out and sent them home to bed," Hunt said.

"Just as well. I wouldn't want them to compare you to me, because you would've been second best," Ty called, then gave a subtle tongue wag to the young waitress. He hadn't changed a bit.

Hunt stood and grabbed his younger brother in a headlock, reminiscent of all the times he really would've liked to strangle him. When he let him up, Ty was smiling, as if he knew.

His brother's hair was longer than when he'd seen him last, his skin tanned from all the time spent outside on the bike, drifting from place to place and doing who knows what. He didn't ask and Ty didn't offer, and Hunt knew better than anyone the line between legal and barely so.

He'd straddled that line himself too many times to count, but he had the US Military backing him. It was a world Ty would never have survived in, although his brother was more of a survivor than anyone truly knew.

"You look good. Not so military." Ty slapped him on the back and Hunt settled into the seat across from him.

"I see you got a new baby." Hunt pointed to the bike through the window, and Ty smiled.

"She's a beauty. I gambled and won her up in Chattanooga."

"I didn't know there was much gambling that way."

"There's more up that way than you could ever dream of, all of it trouble."

"And you find it, I'm sure."

"Trouble finds me," Ty protested. Then he winked at the waitress who'd come over to take his order, and no doubt, to get another look at him. They almost started kissing right in front of Hunt, and he had to stop Ty from following her into the kitchen.

"So, Jon, how's it going? Still living like a monk?" Ty asked, after mouthing, *later,* to the waitress.

Hunt grinned because it had been a long time since anyone had used his real first name. Meaning, it had been too long between visits with Ty. "Why are you so interested in my sex life?"

"Not your sex life. Your love life, as in, are you living alone, like a monk? Getting laid's never been your problem."

Hunt smirked. "I wasn't aware that I had any problems, other than keeping your ass in line."

"Nice avoidance technique."

"I learned from the best," Hunt said, and sighed inwardly. He wondered when his little brother had managed to add pop psychologist to his list of credentials. Ty had always had an insightful, almost sixth-sense kind of thing going on, sometimes eerily so.

You're going to have to stop referring to him as your little brother. He's twenty-five.

Only three years separated the two, and they did share some similarities. Although, the differences at times were so great that Hunt had to wonder where Ty'd come from. Ty had the same freewheeling spirit as their parents had, and he'd inherited their wanderlust and their openness. Their trusting natures.

Hunt enjoyed his travels with the SEALs, but always liked having someplace steady to hang his hat when he came home. Instability in two- to four-month stints in his job, he could handle. In his life, not so much.

Forget about trust. Hunt was always out of there long before any relationship reached that stage, and he never gave out enough personal information to worry. "What about you, Ty? Find the old ball and chain?"

Ty laughed a deep sound that bounced off the walls of

the nearly empty diner and reverberated. The waitress smiled. Ty was infectious that way, always managing to pull everyone into his good time. "Not yet, but I'll know her when I see her."

"Still a romantic."

"I guess so." Ty put salt and ketchup on his eggs and began to chew like he hadn't eaten in weeks. "This place is as good as I remembered. And a long ride always gets my appetite up."

"Yeah, I know what you mean." Hunt dug into his own breakfast.

"You busy today? I thought maybe we'd take a ride up the coast, check out a few bikes I'm looking into buying this morning," Ty offered.

"Can we do it later on? There's something I've got to take care of first." Hunt had a few things that couldn't be put off. He wasn't going to complete the fantasy for Carly, but he did have his own ideas, plenty of them, and he planned to execute each and every one of them on her gorgeous, lithe body as soon as the time was right.

"Does it involve a woman?" his brother asked.

"None of your damned business."

"That means yes, and that's the only excuse I'll accept."

Hunt changed the subject, asked what he'd wanted to from the second he'd seen Ty. "Speaking of excuses, have you been doing what you're supposed to have been doing?"

"I never do, bro. Thought you knew that by now."

Purposeful avoidance. Hunt stared his brother down with his best cut-the-crap face, knowing he didn't stand a chance.

He didn't—Ty just laughed. "I'll make the trip myself, that way you don't have to rush whatever it is you've got to do. But we are going out tonight?"

"Wouldn't miss it."

"Maybe I'll get to meet this mystery woman you're ditching me for."

"I'm not ditching you. And she's not a mystery woman. I'm just doing her a favor." And, oh yeah, he was going to make her work for that favor.

Except you're the one who's all worked up, dumbass.

He could handle it. He'd been through worse. What doesn't kill you makes you stronger. Besides, she wasn't going to be able to resist him when he came calling, and he *was* going to come calling. He purposely left no way for her to get in touch with him. That would've been too easy for her, too convenient, as if she were pulling all the strings.

"Big surprise," Ty muttered.

"What are you talking about?"

"Whenever you mention *woman* and *favor* in the same sentence, I know what you've done. Found yourself another fixer-upper."

"Huh?"

"You know the phrase love 'em and leave 'em? Well, you're fix 'em and leave 'em. Can't you find a woman without problems? Someone who doesn't need you so much?"

"Carly doesn't have problems." Just fantasies. Hunt took a gulp of juice and told himself that he was in control. He wanted her under his command and he would make sure it stayed that way. Or, that it at least worked out that way. He wasn't going to let her know how hard she'd tumbled him. From the second she'd opened the door, in fact. "She just needs a date for a wedding, so I said I'd—"

"Help her out," Ty finished, shaking his head, and Hunt wondered when he'd gone from big brother in charge to being lectured. "You know, it's your responsibility to save the world on the job. In your own life, you're allowed to enjoy. Let down your guard. Let someone cater to you every once in a while."

Now *that* was a fantasy that Hunt couldn't ever see himself allowing to happen. "It'll be fun. This opportunity presented itself, and I never turn down an opportunity to hang out with a beautiful woman. You of all people should understand that."

"I understand, man. I do. As long as we can spend some time together this week, it's all good. And at least I know it's a wild one."

In a few hours, when the sun came up, Hunt would head over to Carly's. He'd wait for her on the beach he was only just at, and see what happened next. "It's gonna be a wild one for sure."

"Speaking of wild, how was the action you caught recently?"

"Where'd you hear about that?" Hunt demanded, and his mind flashed, not pleasantly, to his most recent mission.

"You just told me." His brother shrugged, and took a slug of coffee.

"I'm fine. Obviously."

"Obviously," Ty repeated. "As always."

"Are we going to fight? Because I'd hate to have to kick your sorry butt tonight." Hunt settled against the booth and Ty shook his head. "Besides," Hunt said, "you're not exactly forthcoming about your cross-country adventures."

"I'll fill you in on all the details, unless you've got somewhere else to be."

"This ought to be good," Hunt muttered. His brother laughed again, and things were back to normal.

THE BREAKFAST RUSH HAD just begun. The sound of plates being collected and tables freshened was a welcome distraction. Thanks to the rising smells of warm bread and hash browns from the kitchen, Ty Huntington's appetite had come to life again. A good sign.

"More coffee, honey?" The waitress on the morning shift gave him a nice, easy smile as she set down what was technically his second order of the day.

"More everything would work for me," he replied, smiling, because she was staring at him with a look he recognized well. And, if it weren't so crowded, if it was even a month earlier, he might've whispered for her to meet him in the back of the restaurant. Because that would've been so simple to do. So easy. As it was, having his brother there had saved him from having to turn down the other waitress's offer of a quick pick-me-up.

She waggled a finger at him, still flirting as she gave a mock pout. "You bad boys are all the same."

"No one even comes close to me, sugar. Trust me on that," he said.

Ty took another slug of coffee and decided that putting off the trip up the coast for another day or so wasn't going to matter for now. He'd spend more time relaxing, and if he could wrestle the bike away from his brother later, he'd do a little maintenance.

He'd rebuilt the hog for Jon three years ago, as a birthday present. Not much for someone who'd done so much for him, but Jon never asked for anything in return, aside from the odd, usually small favor now and again.

As much as he'd wanted to spend time with his brother today, Ty had been more than glad when he'd said he was busy. This trip wouldn't be easy, and he'd never taken the easy way out ever, but this time, he wished he could.

On the long ride in from Tallahassee, he'd rehearsed over and over what he was going to tell Jon. And then he'd lost his nerve when he saw him, because the part of Ty that always wanted to protect his older brother whispered, *he doesn't need to know anything right now. Nothing's going to change, one way or the other.*

Ty had thought about not telling his brother at all. Avoidance for that long a time would be easy, but it wouldn't be fair.

It helped that they'd at least gotten along this time. Ty had regaled his older brother with stories of traveling the open road and it was good to see Jon laugh.

He'd like to see a woman do that for Jon. Ty wanted to see his brother all taken care of, but he knew that would require a damned special woman. Jon was stubborn as hell about letting anyone in.

Not like you.

Ty had watched a good friend get hitched before he'd made the trip here, stood up as a witness in front of God and the preacher and it damn nearly broke him. He'd been through all kinds of women, short and tall, every hair color, the tough biker chick and the sweet innocent, and all of them had only wanted the bad boy.

Now's a great time for you to prove you're something more than that.

His appetite faltered, but he forced himself to continue eating. He'd finish his eggs and work on his hog, because both of those things were simple. Everything else he'd worry about later.

7

CARLY'S SISTER'S VOICE, normally screechy when she wasn't being bridezilla, was downright shrill, and Carly had been barely awake when she'd grabbed the phone. The only reason she'd picked it up was because she'd thought it might be Sam, needing to cry on her proverbial shoulder again.

"You're bringing a Navy SEAL to my wedding?" Nicole blurted.

Carly was not thinking it might be Hunt when she'd answered. She had not been dreaming about his big hands all over her or wishing his tongue had found her...

"Is he going to wear camouflage to my wedding? Because Mother said he was wearing camouflage yesterday when she and Dad met him at your house."

"Nicole, he's not..." Definitely not. Because Hunt had disappeared into the night without so much as an, *I'll call you.* Which was a good thing, she told herself firmly as her sister continued to babble on about formal affairs and proper attire.

"He's got to wear a tuxedo to the engagement party. It is a black-tie event."

"Nic..."

"If this is going to be a problem, you need to tell me now," Nicole said. Yes, the problem was that her parents had fueled the rumor mill before Carly had a chance to set things straight with them. And apparently they'd given her sister the full rundown on her new, Navy SEAL boyfriend, who didn't exist. Carly wondered if she should be worried that she couldn't even get a pretend boyfriend to stick around. However, the trouble she'd created was more serious than worrying about Hunt.

Coffee. Lots of strong coffee, preferably in IV-drip form, could get her through this. She struggled out of bed and down the stairs in just her tank top and boy shorts, phone in hand.

Dawn hadn't broken yet. Why was her sister, who could barely drag herself out of bed by noon, up so early?

"I do not need this stress today, Carolyn. I have a full day of wedding plans to go over, and I have a breakfast event of mother's to attend this morning."

"Then don't stress. Hunt's not coming to the wedding."

"Oh." A pause. "So then, you're coming alone? Like a spinster maid of honor?"

Coffee alone was definitely not going to get her through this. Hanging up now might.

Her sister was still talking when Carly clicked the phone off and threw it into the living room. It hit the couch with a less-than-satisfying thud. She abandoned the coffeemaker and headed upstairs for her bathing suit.

She wasn't sure how far she'd get today, but she was not going to let her fear get the best of her forever.

Back downstairs, she walked onto the lanai then stepped onto the sand.

There was a storm brewing and the ocean responded in kind by granting surfers, who were willing to get up this early—the dawn patrol—the thrill of an extra-long ride. She willed herself not to leave, stood close to the spot she and Hunt had used for their interlude. Taking a deep breath, she was prepared to at least be able to walk to that place beyond the dunes where he'd held her close. But she choked up and bailed the second she saw the choppy swells. The rushing tide and the merging clouds distorted everything. The fantasy that had seemed perfect by moonlight was replaced by that familiar fear she despised. She turned her back to the water.

It wasn't going to happen today. Whatever magic Hunt used to get her past the dunes he'd taken with him when he'd disappeared into the night.

When had she gotten so dramatic?

Carly kicked some sand in frustration and stepped slowly toward her house. It had become the long walk of shame she'd come to know so well. As she got closer, she glimpsed a strong, broad back bending over one of the longboards she kept propped against the side of the house.

Hunt.

He'd taken her oldest, and once most-treasured stick and laid it across the patio table. He was using sex wax to rough the board up for riding, giving it all the TLC she hadn't over the past months.

Had he seen her freeze up by the dunes?

"Hey," she said. Carly looked beyond him, down the path that led to the side of her house, and saw his motorcycle parked in the middle of the driveway.

"You're up early," Hunt said without bothering to turn around. She took that opportunity to stare at him, long and hard. He'd stripped off his shirt, and she watched the lean muscles in his back and arms move as he worked the board.

"I'm always up early." She tried to keep her voice steady. "Have you been here long?"

DID YOU SEE ME FREAK OUT? That was what Carly wanted to know.

Indeed, Hunt had seen her panic attack. From the looks of it, the walk down to the dunes was something of a ritual for her, and one that she wasn't happy about.

Her shoulders had tensed, fists clenched, the fear palpable. It made him want to run to her and hug her.

Okay, he wanted to do a lot more than just that, but he could easily recognize someone who needed comfort. He could also recognize when someone wanted to let something go, and not have it be noticed. He could do that, too. "I haven't been here long at all," he replied.

"What are you doing?"

"I wanted to see if Candy Valentine could come out and play."

"She's busy. Very busy."

"I'll bet." He walked over to her, cupped her chin in his hand for a second and then released it. It could've been the sunlight, but he would have sworn he saw a flash of disappointment in her eyes. "Catch any waves this morning?"

"Too choppy for a decent ride, and I don't like wasting time," she lied.

He nodded, went back to roughing up the board. Judging by the erosion of the wax, it hadn't been touched in a while.

Maybe she has other boards she uses. Stop jumping to conclusions.

"Did you surf much around Mayport when you were growing up?" he asked. The beaches around the base were always teeming with surfers. He'd always wanted to catch a few rides himself, but it was always too close to one mission or another, and his CO's warnings of, *hurt yourself doing something stupid and I'll make sure you hurt,* stayed solidly in his mind.

Bad enough he rode the motorcycle without a helmet. His Senior Chief was on his back constantly about that one.

"Some. We mainly went there to check out the guys." She put her tongue against her cheek and then gave him a wicked smile.

"I didn't know jarheads were your type, surfer girl."

"There's a lot you don't know about me, sailor-boy."

"I'd much prefer the nickname Frogman." Damn, he should've gone for that extra-long run he'd promised himself. It might've exorcized some of this pent-up energy…or kicked things up a thousand times worse.

Because that bikini Carly was wearing left nothing to the imagination. Seeing her half naked in the moonlight had been amazing, but seeing her full-out, tanned and gorgeous in the sunlight, hair waving around her face, the micro bottoms of the bikini skimming her hips and the curve of her ass, was throwing him far over the edge.

He thought about cooling off in the ocean, but he didn't want to leave her side. And she didn't seem to mind that he was fired up.

She's merely relieved you're not mentioning her mini-breakdown.

He reached an arm around her waist to pull her close against him. Her skin was warm, the contact intense and within seconds he knew there was no other option but to kiss her.

He pressed his mouth to hers and her tongue played against his. Her fingers gripped his shoulders, as if she wasn't sure if she was going to pull back or not.

He didn't give her that option. With both arms securely

around her back, he continued the kiss until she gave up the fight. Her hands moved up to twist in his hair while his hands caressed her back, playing with the ties of her bikini top.

What he wouldn't give to loosen the strings. He could put his mouth to her nipple, like he did last night—tug the hard bud between his teeth and tongue, make her come from just that and the pressure of a hand stroking between her legs.

The pressure mounted for him—he was impossibly hard, his arousal pressing into her sex through the fabric of their bathing suits. Her hand moved from his shoulder to his back, her nails dragging down lightly over his skin in a way that made his entire body tingle. He rocked against her lightly, the friction nearly enough to send him over the edge.

She whimpered against his mouth and he let his hand drift away from her breasts and down her hip. Broad daylight was getting just a little too bright and populated for the way they were kissing and he was hoping beyond hope that she'd break away and guide him back toward the house. He wasn't going to be the one to give in first.

But when she finally did pull back, it was with a "Hunt, I can't…"

She didn't elaborate any further and he didn't force the issue.

"Is there any of that cake left?" he asked, and walked past her into the house before she had a chance to say another word.

HE'D COME BACK. THAT HAD to be a good sign, had to mean he was going to come to the wedding with her. Although, after her sister's phone performance, Carly was ready to send Hunt to the festivities by himself and run for cover.

Of course, it meant she'd have to cop to the fantasy. But what could be safer than spending time with a Navy SEAL, in bed and out?

She thought about the way he'd stroked her last night and kissed her just now, hard enough to make her beg, and knew there were far more dangerous things. Was it too late to turn back, despite what she'd told Nicole this morning? She'd emailed Evan late last night and told him about Hunt, because if she was going to lie, she was going all the way. She hadn't received Evan's reply yet.

She sighed and went into the house, and heard Hunt talking to himself.

Scratch that. He was talking on the phone. Her phone.

"I have dress whites," he said, and then listened for a second. "Yes, like on JAG."

Oh Lord, he was on the phone with her sister. And doing a fine job of soothing the savage beast with the combo Jedi-SEAL mind-control thing.

"Yes, it photographs well." He listened again. "When is it? Well, sure, bachelor parties are cool."

She grabbed the phone. "Nicole…"

"He doesn't sound military. Daddy still thinks his family's in oil. I don't know why he's with you, but try not to let him dump you before the wedding," Nicole sniffed haughtily before hanging up on *her* this time.

"She seems interesting in a high-strung kind of way." Hunt sat on her counter and put his feet up on the back of one of her chairs.

"You have no idea."

"I'm invited to the bachelor party," he said. "Doesn't sound like it's going to be much fun."

"None of this is going to be any fun." But it wouldn't be much worse if she didn't bring him.

She wished her stomach hadn't flittered nervously when she'd seen him this morning. She wished he hadn't occupied every last one of her dreams, wished he hadn't seen her near-breakdown at the beach and wished, for the final time, that she'd never sent that stupid fax. She hated being boxed in like this.

What were her choices? It was either take Hunt with her, or deal with the fallout. And with Evan and her parents' matchmaking and her sister's whining... She didn't have the time or the energy to focus on all of that. She needed back in the water.

She needed Hunt because he was going to make things easier. And so, the decision was made, at least on her end. "So you'll go to the wedding with me? And the party and the rehearsal dinner, too?"

He gave a casual shrug. "I've got a few conditions."

Yeah, he was going to make it *really* easy. "I can imagine what those might be."

"You know one of them already." He caught his tongue in his cheek and gave her a long, leisurely once-over. "But I'm not going to push that. You want more of the fantasy, you'll tell me the rest of it. I know you will, sooner than later."

She wondered how he got that ego through the door. "So let me get this straight. You're not going to try anything, but somehow you think I'll try and seduce you?"

"Yep."

No way was he going to win that bet, but it got her off the hook. Momentarily, anyway, because he seemed to have another condition.

She headed to the sink, her throat suddenly dry, and filled a large glass with water. She took a sip before she spoke again. "What's the second thing you want?"

"I want you to teach me how to surf."

The glass slipped out of her hand, shattering into a million pieces against the ceramic-tile floor, and she wished she could join it there.

There was no picking up the pieces.

8

HUNT WAS NEXT TO HER IN a second, moving her away from the mess. "You're not wearing shoes. I've got it," he said gently, because the look in her eyes was somewhere between faraway and beyond reaching, and he did not like that look.

She sat quietly in a chair, watching him sweep up the broken glass with a broom that she'd pointed him to. "I'm just tired. That always makes me clumsy," she said weakly. "Not eating this morning didn't help."

"Probably not," he agreed. He emptied the glass pieces into her garbage and then took her wrist in his hand and put a thumb on her pulse.

"I'm fine," she insisted. And she did appear better, more focused. There was some color in her cheeks. "Am I going to live, Doctor Huntington?"

"Funny girl. Just sit there. I'll make you breakfast," he said. He found the makings for scrambled eggs and toast in her fridge. While he prepared the food, he turned to the stove to give her a little extra time to pull herself together. Because his suspicions had been confirmed, although he wished, for her sake, they hadn't been.

Carly Winters was scared to go in the water.

At least she was still trying. The fact that she went down by the water meant something, meant she still had that fire. She might be afraid, but she wasn't letting it rule her completely. She had to get back on the horse, or she'd never forgive herself.

He set the eggs and toast in front of her even as she insisted he didn't need to go to any more trouble for her. But she didn't hesitate to start eating, and after she'd finished most of what was on her plate, he knew it was time to push it a little further. He'd only known her a very short while, but the sense of strength he'd gotten from her wasn't in his imagination. She could handle it.

"So, do we have a deal?" he asked.

"A deal?"

"I'll be your date for the wedding and for all the other parties over the next couple of weeks, and you can teach me how to surf."

"And you really want nothing else in return?" she asked.

His mind flashed back to last night, to the way her moans echoed in his ear if he thought hard enough. He could still smell the coconut, the beach and her. He wanted nothing more than to grab Carly and put her across his lap, strip her down and lick every last inch of her.

But he was damned if he was going to be the one to make the next move. It was her fantasy, and she had to want it, to. And she did want it. It was like a big game of chicken now, and he'd hold steady and wait to see her next move.

"I told you, the fantasy's up to you. I've never had to force a woman to do something she doesn't want to do." He brushed some hair from her face, touched her cheek lightly with the back of his hand. Warm from the sun, her skin was sun-kissed in that irresistible, natural surfer girl way. So tempting. "Do we have a deal?"

"Yes." Her voice was barely a whisper, and he swore she'd leaned in toward him, imperceptibly, and he braced himself for a kiss, a touch from her, anything.

A rolling boom of thunder shook the windows as the sky opened to break their moment. She pulled back, sighed, and he took his hand away.

"Well then," she said, "we've got some work to do."

"Yes, we do." He hadn't moved. In fact, he'd stayed as close as possible without actually touching her, and he did want to touch her.

Damn, she was pretty. He'd bet his next paycheck that she had another tattoo somewhere on her body. They were addictive, and most people couldn't stop with one.

Carly didn't seem as if she'd let anything stop her, ever, but he understood fear well. On the job, it was an emotion he let work for him, rather than against him. Fear meant he was still alive when adrenaline was pounding so fast he could barely breathe. And thinking was out of the question because he had to move, or fire, or get the hell out of Dodge. Fear could be paralyzing, but he hadn't let it win yet.

"Not *that* kind of work," she said. "We've got to get to know each other. You told my parents we'd been dating for six months."

"Dating sucks and men are pigs," a female voice called out. Hunt turned to see who had uttered such revealing words. Carly giggled.

The owner of the *men are pigs* comment was wearing a simple sundress, her dark hair in a ponytail. She was really cute and curvy. And she was carrying a box of donuts, so he figured she couldn't be all bad.

"Oh, shoot," the woman said, coming to a dead halt when she spied the two of them. "Sorry, I didn't realize you had company, or I would've kept my mouth shut," she said. "I'm Carly's friend Samantha. But you can call me Sam. Everyone does."

"I'm Hunt," he said, and he let her earlier comments go.

"I brought breakfast." Sam held out the donuts.

"I already ate, but Hunt didn't," Carly said. She hadn't moved from her chair, and an eye kept watch on the storm outside. The tops of the palm trees swaying was visible through the sliding glass doors.

"It's a fast-moving storm. It'll break soon," Hunt told them, and Carly looked at him with a small smile.

"Are you all right?" Samantha asked Carly.

"I'm a bit wound up. I didn't get much sleep last night." She glanced at him quickly, as though she'd admitted more than she'd wanted to in front of him.

That makes two of us who tossed and turned last night.

"He's the one who got the fax?" asked Sam, and Carly nodded and blushed.

Hunt put two and two together and figured this must be the one who was trying to liven up her sex life. From the sounds of it, that hadn't worked out too well.

"Carly told me you are in the Navy," Sam was saying. "Do you live here? I mean, are you stationed around here?"

"No. My team's out of Virginia. I'm here to catch up with my brother," he explained. "I'm supposed to go out with him tonight. Why don't you both come along?"

"Sam and I are staying in tonight, since she's got work in the morning," Carly said.

"But going out with you and your brother sounds much more fun," Sam contradicted. "And after dealing with one hundred sixteen year olds five days straight, I could use a night out."

"Parole officer?"

"High school teacher."

"Same thing, where I came from," he said, and he was sure there were more than a few boys in her class with a crush on the teacher. "Do you need a ride?"

"I'm not sure if we can make it," Carly said quickly. Too quickly. As if she was backing out of the deal as fast as she could.

"I'd really like to see you tonight, Carly," he said.

"We'll meet you," Sam offered, and he grinned at the way she ignored the look of death Carly sent her.

"I'll be at Magee's all night," he said on his way out, taking a donut from Sam's box. By the time he reached the front door, the patter of rain on the roof had stopped and the sky opened up, blue as anything.

DAY TWO, AND Hunt had managed to leave Carly with his self-restraint barely intact. Sooner or later, the lid would blow off, but for now, it was definitely time for that run.

He rode a few miles to the public beach, parked, and stripped down to his shorts. Because there was nothing like running on the beach, especially when his CO wasn't barking up his ass, threatening to cut off vital body parts.

No, a nice, long, lazy run was much better, bare feet pounding the wet sand, calf muscles stretching taut and aching with every step. For the first half, Hunt allowed his mind to clear and stay on autopilot. Vaguely aware of the ocean on his right, and the tourists baking in the last of the sun to his left, it was just hot enough, but there was the promise of a cooler evening. Maybe even some rain, which kept him moving.

Six miles up the beach and Carly entered his mind. And

she refused to leave, too, even when he purposefully checked out other bikini-clad women trolling the beach and the boardwalk.

No one looked like Carly in that tiny, blue-and-white striped bikini with the flimsy string ties on each hip. He could easily see himself untying them with his teeth, pictured her smiling down at him, her hands in his hair…

Hope the water's cold.

He hit it at full speed, dove under the first rolling wave he saw and stayed under as long as he could. When he surfaced, he swam past the breakers until he came to smoother waters. The current helped push him along toward the beach that surrounded Carly's place.

How had he gotten so wrapped up in her so quickly? Ty was right about the women he usually picked, but Carly was different. He didn't want to just help her. He just wanted more.

Meanwhile, she'd handed him a real challenge. And a SEAL was always up for a challenge.

THE THING ABOUT BEST friends was that you couldn't lie to them. Carly could try, certainly, but it wouldn't do any good. Sam's radar was honed on years of late-night talks and perfected from teaching kids who'd forgotten more about lying than Carly ever knew.

Still…

"We were not about to have sex on the kitchen table," Carly protested. *We probably would've started out in the chair.*

Sam eyed her. "Just finished, then?"

"I think you've been reading too much Candy Valentine."

"Or, if my last night is any indication, not enough. At

least now I know why I had to leave a message the first time I called. You've got an amazing excuse."

"Hunt didn't spend the night. We were taking a walk on the beach." Carly felt the blood rush straight to her breasts at the thought of the way he'd handled them last night. She brought her knees up to her chest, balancing her heels on the edge of the wooden kitchen chair. "Are you feeling better today?"

She and Sam had already spent over an hour on the phone, pre-dawn. During one of Carly's toss-and-turn, maybe-some-cake-will-help-me-sleep moments, she'd seen the blinking message light and had immediately called her friend. As she'd suspected, Sam was awake and in need of comfort. At the time, Carly had put off telling her much about Hunt, mainly because she was too mixed up to even begin to sort out what had happened.

"I'll live." She pulled out a chair and sat next to Carly, "I know I'm better off without him. And a man like Hunt could make me a believer again."

"Um, well…"

"I'm teasing. I know he's taken."

"He's not taken. He's helping me out of a jam." It was her turn to explain to her friend the previous night's events, and Sam's jaw dropped.

"He met your parents?"

"Can you imagine what the next two weeks are going to be like, Sam?" Carly buried her face in her knees.

"You like him, don't you?"

"*You* like him."

"Yeah, who wouldn't? But he's into you."

"He's into me, all right. And he's on to me too," she mumbled.

"Are you going to bring him to the wedding?"

"I don't think I have a choice, if I want to keep my family off my back."

"Imagine, all this happened because of one innocent fax," Sam mused.

"A not-so-innocent fax, and it's all your fault," Carly reminded her.

"Are you sure I won't be interrupting anything tonight if I come along to Magee's?"

"He's my stand-in wedding date, not my real one."

"Uh-huh. Well, in that case, consider this an adventure. A big, camouflaged adventure." Sam paused. "Something else is wrong."

"I still haven't been able to get close to the water," she admitted.

Sam put her hand on Carly's arm. "What can I do to help?"

"I don't think anybody can help. I think it's something I have to do alone," she said. "Except that Hunt wants me to give him surfing lessons in exchange for taking him to the wedding."

"Oh, boy." Sam sighed. "Did you tell him you can't?"

"No, because I'm hoping I can."

Her friend looked thoughtful. "You know, this might be the best thing for you."

"Someone to humiliate me?"

"Someone to help you light your fire. Sexually and otherwise. I know you haven't had sex since the accident. And you'd been in a dry spell before that."

It was true. Right before the accident, she'd thrown herself into non-stop training, and so had Dan. And even though exercise was supposed to be a natural aphrodisiac to up the sex drive, things had been going downhill in their relationship fast. Dan was far more interested in hanging out with his buddies. For Carly, the idea of a night with him was five minutes of pleasure, definite for him and maybe for her if she hurried, and then he'd be gone.

She'd ended up channeling all her desire into winning. It didn't keep her warm at night, but she hadn't realized how much she missed the sexual contact until Hunt showed up at her door. "How nice of you to keep track," Carly said.

Sam ignored her. "Maybe, if you got your passion back in your love life, you'd get your passion back for surfing."

"It's not passion for surfing I'm missing," she said, but Sam merely shrugged.

"Sometimes passion makes us override our fears."

"For a woman who just broke up last night, you sound amazingly calm. And far too wise for…" Carly glanced up at the clock for the time. "Hey, doesn't your first class start in like ten minutes?"

"Shoot, I'll be late and I hate being late." Sam jumped up and grabbed a donut. "Keep trying to go to the water. And maybe there's something to the surfing lesson thing. Maybe having Hunt with you will make it easier."

Nothing was getting easier with Hunt around. Things seemed to be growing more and more complicated, and Carly wondered if they'd ever be simple again.

9

EARLY EVENING IN southern Florida brought a gorgeous orange sunset mixed with yellow, worthy of the old saying, *red sky at night, sailor's delight.* Carly hadn't made it back down to the water, and to be fair, she hadn't even tried.

The bath to soothe her muscles had turned into an extra-long soak in the tub, thanks to a certain man in uniform she couldn't seem to tear from her thoughts. She'd stretched contentedly in the warm water, had let her hand slide between her legs and heard Hunt's voice the way it had sounded last night, rough against her ear, urging her to *let go, baby.* How she wanted his hands on her. If she'd had his phone number, she'd have been calling him, maybe talking dirty to him while she ran the washcloth over her nipples, pretending it was his tongue, demanding he come right over to make her come.

And then she'd been jelly, because two orgasms in two days was more than she'd had in months. She'd forgotten how good it felt. When it was with the correct person. And Hunt had certainly done everything correctly.

Once she'd had enough bath-time fantasyland, she'd spent the better part of the afternoon playing around with, and ultimately procrastinating about her next article. Her piece was due Monday. Although she had managed to get ahold of the person she needed to interview—an up-and-coming surfer who'd recently won his first major competition after a massive wipe-out in an early heat.

Dude, I like went over the falls and totally pearled.

"Yeah, dude, like, me too," she murmured, and considered another bath as she crumpled the notes about surfer slang and culture. She threw the ball of paper toward the wastepaper basket just as the phone began to ring. Probably sponsors responding to the last-minute invitations she'd sent for the charity benefit.

"Carolyn? Where have you been? Don't you return messages?" Nicole asked.

When she heard her sister's voice, Carly made a solemn vow to always let the machine answer. "What's up?"

"What's up is that your dress is in. And you're going to need an expert tailor to fit it to you, because I'm sure it's going to be much too big on top."

Okay, that was probably true, but it was totally unnecessary for Nicole to point out. "I'll take care of it right away," she said.

"Yes, but you can't take it into any dry cleaners to have it fixed. The top has a tulle overlay. It's delicate. And I had to get this particular dress, rather than the one I wanted because Mother said I needed to choose something that would cover the scar on your back."

"Just bite me, Nic."

"Nice language. Anyway, Mother and I think you should come here to get the dress fitted properly."

"Fine," she said through clenched teeth. Again, useless to argue. Think Zen thoughts. "Let me know when."

"Tomorrow. Noon. And then we'll have lunch."

"And suppose tomorrow isn't good for me?" she asked.

"I *am* the one getting married next week. You're supposed to be catering to my whims. Besides, if you don't come tomorrow, the seamstress can't promise that the dress will be ready in time."

"I'll be there, then."

"And you need to wear something formal to the engagement party. Mother said that if you don't have anything appropriate, she'll take you shopping tomorrow after lunch."

"I've already got my flip-flops picked out." She heard the gasp of horror on the other end of the phone and wondered if she'd been adopted. "It's a joke. And no, I don't need any help getting ready for the party. I've got something you'll approve of."

"Good. Oh, by the way, everyone's very interested in your new boyfriend," Nicole said.

"How did everyone hear about my new boyfriend?"

"I told them."

Carly clutched the receiver hard and pretended it was Nicole's throat as her sister continued.

"They asked how you guys met and I told them that I was sure you'd give us all the details at the party. I mean, it's been so long since you've brought a date anywhere and people are curious, especially about the fact that you'd give up someone like Evan—"

"Evan and I were never dating—"

"—for a soldier."

"He's a sailor, technically."

"Whatever. Either way, people are interested."

I'll just bet. "Nicole, I've got to go. I'll see you tomorrow." Carly hung up the phone, sank into the couch and reviewed her options. Because, as of one hour ago, she'd told herself she wasn't going to search out Hunt tonight, and she wasn't going to take him up on any offer.

Now, she had to go to Magee's and take some time to get their story straight. It would be more than Carly could endure to have her "boyfriend" outed as a sham in the middle of the party. Some maid of honor she'd be.

"I'M *SO* NOT GOING IN THERE," Sam said, as she eyed the bar from the safety of the cab while Carly paid the driver.

It was very like Samantha to change her tune when they actually arrived at the bar, so Carly had at least been mentally prepared for the breakdown. "You were the one who used the line, big camouflaged adventure, remember?" she prodded her friend. "We could go back, though."

She hoped Sam wouldn't make her turn around, since Carly had already come up with a thousand different deals she could make with Hunt, and picked the most plausible one. She'd offer to tell him the fantasy in place of surfing lessons. She'd tell him she was too busy or didn't have the patience anymore to teach. Most men would take sex over surfing lessons.

Granted, Hunt wasn't most men, but she knew what he wanted. Mainly, because she wanted the same thing.

Sam sighed. "All right. We've come this far, and I'm tired of moping. I've been moping through the entire relationship. And really, nothing could possibly be as bad as last night was for me, right?"

Carly had the opposite problem, and wondered if Hunt could possibly be as good as he was last night. Because, if he was, she was this close to revealing her Candy Valentine side to her pretend serious boyfriend.

"I promise, you'll have fun," Carly said. She grabbed her friend's arm and they walked past the row of motorcycles that lined the parking lot. There was a bit of a line, but she and Sam got smiles and winks from the bouncers, and found themselves inside the bar pretty quickly.

"It's packed," she heard Sam say, but Carly had paused at the edge of the dance floor, half of which extended out of the open-walled bar and onto the beach.

There's a ton of beach between this place and the water. So take a breath.

"Do you see him?" Sam asked, tugging her arm to move her forward. Carly scanned the bar first and then her eye moved to the tables. No luck. And then she caught sight of Hunt, too close to the water for her comfort and in the company of three women. Three very pretty, very young women who smiled and laughed at whatever he was saying.

He's not that *funny.* "He's over there. By the water," Carly said, careful not to point in his direction.

"He's surrounded. And looks awfully happy about it," Sam said.

"Thanks. Just remember, you were the one who told him we'd come here and you're the one who talked me into this."

"Are you jealous?"

"He's my *stand-in* boyfriend." Still, the urge to cut across the dance floor came with a sense of propriety that surprised her.

"Aren't you going to say hi?"

"He can come to me," Carly said and Sam laughed.

"Playing hard to get with your *stand-in,* huh? Okay, no problem. Let's get some drinks then."

They found stools at the bar since most people were dancing or on the beach. Sam ordered drinks and started talking to a guy who approached her while Carly leaned against the back of the stool and got comfortable. Carly was glad at least some good could come out of this mess she'd made. Her friend deserved to have fun.

"I know you're waiting for someone, but do you mind my company?"

She turned to find a handsome man, with blond hair longer than Hunt's pulled back at his neck. He was tan, which made his neon blue eyes stand out, and she was going to invite Sam in on the conversation when her friend whispered, "Camouflaged adventure at six o'clock."

So Hunt had finally torn himself away from his adoring public. Well, two could play at this game. "I'm Carly."

"I'm Cash," the handsome guy said.

"What makes you think I'm waiting for someone?"

"You're too damned gorgeous not to be taken. Unless it's my lucky night." He smiled, leaned in toward her. "What's your pleasure?"

"She's here to see me," Hunt's voice interrupted.

"I didn't see her with you. And why the hell would you leave her alone, anyway?" Cash asked. And it was immediately obvious that the two men knew each other.

"Maybe you could arm wrestle for my attention." Carly was enjoying the bid for her time. After seeing Hunt surrounded by women, she needed to gain back a little bit of leverage.

"I've already gotten your attention, and I don't plan on letting it go," Hunt said, then stepped in front of Cash and gave her a once over that made her blush. Dammit all if she didn't want to melt into him.

"Hasn't anyone taught you that it's rude to stare?" she asked, knowing full well she'd dressed this way because she wanted him to do more than stare.

She'd worn a semi-sheer empire-style tank top, paired it with an older, broken-in pair of jeans cut raggedly to mid-calf and she'd put on a touch of make-up, mostly around her eyes. One last glance in the mirror to run a brush through her hair and she'd been done. Her mother and sister would've never agreed with that statement, since her hair tumbled wildly past her shoulders, but it was her all the way.

"People have been trying to teach me things for years, but I'm not easily trained." He paused. "For you, I'd be willing to go try, though."

"Really, now?" It was her turn to give him a once over, and he didn't seem to mind. In his well-worn Levi's and white T-shirt, with the ever-present flip-flops and hair hanging over his forehead, he looked like the best beach bum she'd ever seen. And that was no mean feat, considering he was standing next to a handsome guy, who hadn't even pulled her thoughts from Hunt for a second. And she didn't want to stop and analyze what that meant. "What kind of training?"

"On a surfboard, Carly. You do have an awfully dirty mind, don't you?"

"Are you two going to get a room or what?" Cash asked as he looked between the two of them.

"You must be Hunt's brother," she said, although aside from the blond hair, she didn't see many similarities.

"Teammate," Hunt said to her, and to Cash, "I thought you were working? I thought you were behind on paperwork?"

"I got bored." Cash ordered a few beers, handed one to Carly and one to Hunt. "Here's to *not* leaving beautiful women waiting," he said pointedly, and Hunt just glared at him.

"He's always looking for the next beautiful woman," Hunt told her.

"Don't believe him," Cash said. "He's simply not up for the competition." Like Hunt had earlier, he seemed to have no problem attracting his fair share of attention from other women in the bar. In fact, they were slowly starting to circle him, and his attention wandered toward them.

"I thought Jason wasn't letting you start your R&R until you finished that paperwork?" Hunt asked Cash again, who was busy making eye contact with a tall redhead.

"He won't even notice I'm gone," he scoffed.

"Hey, Cash?"

"Yeah?"

"I think he noticed." Hunt motioned to a man who was barreling toward them at an alarmingly fast rate, despite the number of people. He looked taller than Hunt, which meant he had to be over six foot three. Cash was slightly shorter than Hunt, and leaner, too, and she wondered if he'd have a shot against the living, breathing tank headed in their direction. Cash swore under his breath and disappeared into the crowd. Carly noticed he managed to snag the redhead on the way.

"Sorry about that," Hunt said. "Jason's my CO. I've got to remember to thank him for corralling Cash."

"So, you're really not up for the competition."

"I'm up for anything, but I think you already knew that," he said.

Her stomach tightened because yes, she knew.

"But I'd never have taken you for the jealous type."

"What are you talking about?" she asked.

"Why didn't you come over and say hi when you got here?"

She should've known he wouldn't have missed her. "You were busy."

"Now, who's not up for competition?" He sat forward as if he was going to kiss her and yes, she wanted him to. Right here, right now.

"That's a sweet tattoo."

Hunt groaned and pulled back, because another guy had come up from behind him and pointed to her ankle. And then he started to run his finger over the swirls of gray and blue, tracing the outline of the fin. "Colors are deep. You probably won't have to have this retouched for a long time. But when you do, I know a place."

Hunt sighed. "*This* is my brother. Ty, this is Carly."

Dark to Hunt's blond, Ty was Hunt's height and good-looking, as well. "You get the tat done around here?" he asked.

She shook her head. "Hawaii. After my first final in a competition." The beginning of the glory days, when her biggest care in the world was waxing her board and lying in the sun all afternoon once the surf had wrung her out.

"Ah, right. Hunt mentioned you were a surfer girl. Is that like a surfing tradition?" Ty asked, and she wondered what else Hunt had mentioned.

"It's more like an unwritten, do something after you've been circled by your first shark, tradition. At least in my surfing circle."

"I love a good shark story," Hunt said. "Don't be shy." He slung an arm across the back of her seat, while Ty propped up the bar and waited for her story.

She didn't need much coaxing, especially because the story was one of her favorites. "Well, it was my first run of the event," she said. "I paddled out, hung around with a few other buddies for a while, waiting to catch that great wave of the morning. My friends took off when the waves started rolling in, but I was looking for something bigger."

Hunt grinned, a wide, easy gesture. She rolled her eyes at him and continued. "It's not like you can surf for any amount of time and not see a shark, but they're usually far enough away that it's not a problem." She thought back to that day, all blue sky and smooth-as-glass water and that catch-in-your-throat feeling when she'd seen the fin. "It was close. Maybe three feet by the time I spotted it, but I'd been so intent on the surf that I hadn't bothered to look around the way I'd been taught."

"Tiger shark?" Hunt asked.

"Had to be, the way it zoomed up to me and started circling. I put my legs up on the board and prayed for balance. But he wasn't leaving, and his circle was getting tighter and tighter."

She remembered her throat closing up in terror, her inability to scream, but also the sheer amazement at being close to something that cool.

One of the perks of being eighteen and stupid. Very stupid.

"What'd you do?" Ty prodded.

"I'd planned to sit there and wait him out. But then I caught sight of this hollow coming up from behind me." The hollow that had held the promise of the perfect wave, the curl angling exactly right, the bump beginning off her left shoulder and growing.

"I was going to miss it if I waited out the damned shark. So I maneuvered onto my stomach and started paddling."

"Holy shit," Hunt muttered, and Ty's eyebrows were raised.

"And the shark was interested, because he followed me for a while, closer once I caught the swell. I was halfway between checking that he didn't get under my board and watching to make sure I caught the swell at the sweet spot."

"Don't stop now, surfer girl," Ty urged.

She'd forgotten how a good shark story could liven up a room, especially when being told to a group of non-surfers. "The shark was moving faster, and I wasn't sure if it was the current or if it was trying to keep up with me, like it was trying to play a game." She paused. "One of the best rides of my life. I rode out the tube like nobody's business."

"And the shark?" Ty asked.

"He followed me in the tube for a while, like he'd caught the perfect ride, too. I concentrated on not wiping out. And by the time I got to the end, no more fin." She smiled. "I got the tattoo that night, in it's honor. If it wasn't for the shark, I'm not sure the ride would've been half the high it was, trophy or no trophy."

Ty laughed and Hunt nodded, as if he understood the term adrenaline rush all too well.

"You're not telling that shark story again, are you?" Sam asked from over her shoulder. Carly quickly introduced Ty to her best friend. "You can call me Sam, everyone does."

"I'm not everyone," Ty said to her, and Carly looked back and saw the blush rise on Sam's face. "And I think it's time for a shot in that shark's honor."

"I think it's time for Carly to come dance with me," Hunt spoke up, and looked pointedly at his brother. "Can I trust you here with Sam?"

She heard her friend sigh quietly from behind her and murmur something about *feeling circled* herself, and Ty merely smiled.

10

"WAS THAT STORY TRUE?" Hunt already had his arms around Carly, swaying her to the low beat coursing through the sound system. He fought the urge to stop talking and start kissing, even though that's all he'd wanted to do from the second he'd seen her walk into the bar. Her cheeks were flushed, her eyes had that slightly glazed look, the look of someone who was having fun and wasn't thinking too hard or too much.

It looked good on her. Really good.

"Are you accusing me of telling a fish tale?" She'd deflected his question with the ease of a trained professional, which he could appreciate.

"Not at all," he replied, and figured that it must've been some wave that rolled her if she could handle a tiger shark without losing it.

"I might have forgotten to mention that that particular shark was kind of a regular out in that surfing spot. Kind of a hanger-on," she admitted.

"I can see how that would take away some of the story's impact. Still, a damned good one."

"I'm sure you've got some tales of your own," she said.

Speaking of tales, he caught a glimpse of Cash heading toward the back exit with the redheaded woman in tow. That his teammate ditched their CO was somewhat surprising. Though Hunt hadn't been sure which man to lay his bet on.

Hunt also knew, from previous experience, that that particular door Cash exited led out to a private stretch of beach, and that Cash wasn't going out there to talk. And since his friend's track record of always picking a woman who was already spoken for was well known, Hunt had a feeling the night was going to be wilder than he'd intended.

"I've got a few stories," he admitted. "Half the time I'm lucky to come out with my ass, and the rest of me, intact. But so far it's all worked out."

"That's good to know," she said.

He felt a touch on his back, and turned to find one of the women he'd been talking to earlier smiling up at him as she passed by. He grinned and looked back at Carly. "Hey, I wasn't sure you were going to show," he said.

"So you were preparing back-up?"

"I was passing the time, not looking to get invited to any more weddings. I'm friendly."

"I noticed. And I wasn't sure I was going to show up, either," she said, a small smile curving her mouth.

If he had his way, which he planned on, she'd be doing a lot more than smiling tonight.

"But I figured we needed to get to know each other."

"That's what I'm doing." He pressed harder against her, trying to memorize every curve of her body with his own, noticing how well she fit next to him. He let his lips brush the lobe of her ear, felt her shiver despite the steam coming from the busy dance floor.

"I meant for the party and the rehearsal dinner. And the wedding. The whole reason for this, remember? As in, get our stories straight so no one suspects."

"What's there to suspect?"

"That we're not together," she murmured, as he made sure they remained very much together for the time being, his arm around her waist, his other hand moving her hips against his in a way that was driving him crazy.

"Let's start by you telling me the end of the fantasy. That's what I really need to know," he said.

"Nice try, but you made the deal, remember?"

"I remember. Doesn't matter. You're going to spill all your intel soon, anyway."

"And if I don't?"

"I'll have to seduce it out of you. And trust me, I'm very well-versed in that art." His thigh slipped between hers, giving a certain amount of pressure. He watched the flush rise on her cheeks.

"Hunt, we're in a public place."

"I know. How do you feel about that? Part of that secret fantasy?"

It was beyond obvious how he felt about it, was lucky that brain damage didn't result from his walking around with a hard-on for so long.

"You're impossible," she whispered.

"Figured you'd like that quality," he said.

"So, I was thinking," she began in an attempt to regain control, but he wasn't about to give away the upper hand that soon.

"Thinking too much is something I try not to do when I'm on leave. Or dancing."

"Partial leave," she reminded him. "I think you'll like this, though. It's about our deal."

"You pulling out?" he asked as he made sure his knee most decidedly did not pull out from its spot between her thighs. And she didn't seem to be complaining.

"Sweetening the pot," she said.

"Now that's more like it."

"How about I give you the fantasy instead of the surf lessons?" she asked.

Her voice held just the right amount of huskiness, the seductive hint of promise he'd been waiting for.

Damn, that was an offer he'd be an idiot to refuse, and that was what she'd been banking on. Which was why he had to refuse and hope it didn't backfire in his face, or else all he'd get out of this was a few boring parties and a surfboard. And really, he did want the sex. Needed the sex. Lots of it, and all of it with Carly. He and Carly on the surfboard.

Pull it together and think. "You know, I'd love nothing better, but I made a bet with Cash that I could learn to surf faster than he could, and I'm not losing face on this one. I've got a pro on my side. You're my ace in the hole." He nuzzled her neck and prayed she bought it.

"So that's why Cash was trying to woo me away from you," she said.

"Among other reasons. But I'm going to win both anyway." He paused. "Now, about that fantasy…"

"Why don't you tell me one of your fantasies instead?"

"Carly, I have a lot of fantasies. And I wouldn't mind playing all of them out with you, so say the word." And yeah, he wanted her to say it right now, because she looked so good, smelled so good and she was so close—he wasn't going to be able to control himself much longer.

"WHY DO I HAVE A FEELING one of your fantasies is sex in a public place?" Carly asked finally, before her imagination carried her too far away.

His hand lingered on her waist, then caressed her lower

back in small circles while his knee continued its slow grind. "Part of the thrill is wondering if you're going to get caught. And I know you like thrills, or you wouldn't have surfed for a living."

"I'm sure you've had your share of thrills. On and off the job," she said, and he nodded slowly, let a grin tug at his mouth and pulled her in even closer.

"You know as well as I do that the best part of the thrill begins here." He pointed to her forehead. And he was right.

"Besides, my job's dangerous," he said. "I try not to think about that aspect of it—I just do it. Same as you, probably. And I'd rather not talk about the job now, unless it's the job I'm going to do for you," he said.

"Part of your job as my boyfriend of six months, your words, not mine, is to share your deepest, darkest secrets with me. So tell me one of your best stories."

"Most of them are classified," he admitted. "And the ones that aren't, you probably wouldn't want to hear about."

"Try me."

"Ever parachuted?"

"I've parasailed."

He shook his head, like it wasn't the same thing at all. "Maybe I'll take you for a nice jump out of a plane and tell you about the time I jumped and my chute didn't open."

"What happened?"

"I had to freefall until my CO caught up with me. We landed. The helo picked us back up and I made the jump again. Right back on the horse, like the saying goes."

"I think I'll stick to water," she said, blatantly ignoring his life's lesson before realizing the irony in her own words. A quick glance toward the rolling ocean over his shoulder in the distance and she brought her gaze to his face. Because tonight, she didn't want to think about surfing. She needed to get him to focus, and fast. "Hunt, we really do have work to do."

"In my experience, you're better off giving as little information as possible. Less talk. Too much talking gets you into trouble. More action is the way to go."

"I know what kind of action you're talking about," she said. His hand threatened to travel lower and she didn't have the desire to stop it.

"I'm saying that if we continue acting like we're together, it'll be more effective than talking about it," he said. "For instance, I'd much rather you *show* me that you can't get enough of me in bed than talk about it."

"Yeah, like I'm going to say that to friends and family."

"You don't have to—that part will come from me."

"You wouldn't dare."

His eyebrows raised. "I think we both know how well I take dares."

She did know. That and several other things about Hunt, like the fact that she'd met him less than forty-eight hours ago and had already come close to revealing things she hadn't told anyone except her very best friend. She felt extremely comfortable, even content, in his arms.

She wasn't sure she wanted to admit that to herself. "I'll come up with the cover story—we can work it out on the drive to the party next week."

"Okay with me," he said.

He was smiling again. His eyes were heavy-lidded and made her want to take off his shirt in the middle of the dance floor and explore every inch of his chest. And then she'd work on his jeans…. "You're really good-looking, you know. I chose my stand-in well," she said.

"You didn't choose me. I saved you. And now I find out that you only like me for my looks."

"Who said anything about needing to be saved? Or liking you?"

"You liked me enough last night," he murmured against her cheek. "If your moans were any indication, I bet you get louder during sex, don't you? You don't seem like you'd hold anything back in bed."

Carly couldn't help but reach out and touch his cheek, then run her fingers along the strong line of his jaw. His lips curved in a grin and she didn't want to think about surfing, or the water, or anything else anymore except the way his lips felt on hers. "Your house isn't soundproofed, is it?"

"That loud?"

"I like to show my appreciation."

"I'd like to show mine, too. I'm hoping you'll let me tonight," he said.

"You're so sure I'll spill my fantasy sooner than later, aren't you?"

"I have to be sure. There are only so many cold showers a man should be forced to take in a twenty-four-hour period."

"And how many have you taken?"

"Let's just say, I've reached my limit." He kissed her then, hard enough to make her forget where they were or anything to do with weddings. She twined her hands in his hair as his tongue played against the roof of her mouth and then with hers. He deepened the kiss as she brought her arms around his shoulders. His thigh pushed between hers again, and when he grabbed her hips, she prayed that no one interrupted them anytime soon.

11

SAM SHIFTED IN HER seat at the bar, cursing the fact that she'd worn the low-cut tank top. Mostly, she was wishing she was home, tucked into bed. Safe and sound. Because there was nothing either safe or sound about Ty. Though Hunt's brother was handsome, she wasn't ready for this—not the bar, the loud music, and least of all, the conversation. She wasn't ready for the newest chase, and Ty certainly made her feel like a conquest.

She didn't need another broken heart. Parting with Joe hadn't come close to devastating her, but this man, with his bad boy swagger and promise of good times and seduction could slay her easily.

When she'd wished for a wild man in her dreams the other night, she'd never expected one to come crashing into her life in vivid, tattooed color.

Surely there were plenty of other women Ty could hit on. She'd let him off the hook and tell him, at the soonest opportunity, that he didn't have to babysit her. And then she'd catch a cab home. Carly would understand.

"So, Samantha, what do you do?" Ty leaned an elbow on the crowded bar, cordoning off an area for her where she wouldn't be bumped. He'd moved her away from the guy she'd been speaking to earlier, gently but firmly, as if he already owned her. His focus was all raw energy and on her alone.

"For a living?" she asked.

"We could start there."

"I'm a teacher." She took a long swig from her beer bottle, and her heart beat a tiny bit faster. She might have imagined it, but she could have sworn he'd moved closer to her.

"Hot for teacher," he said, caressing her forearm.

"Like I've never heard that one before."

"Never from anyone like me. Want to take a ride on my bike?"

"I've never ridden a motorcycle before."

Ty winked. "That's good. I like virgins."

"Are you always this forward?"

"Yes. Always. I go after what I want."

They all did, and she didn't do one-night stands. It was the main reason she'd always gone with the more predictable relationships rather than the take-your-breath-away kind. She'd grown up watching her mother having her breath, and her heart, taken away at the same time. Sam firmly planned on traveling the opposite route.

Boring, yes, but safe. And safe was good. "I'm sure you'll find plenty of women around this place who want you." She made a move to walk away, but he blocked her.

"But I don't want other women."

"Tonight you do."

"Hey, Samantha, wait."

"Cut the crap. I've dealt with bigger and badder than you. I'm having fun, but I'm not into your type, okay?"

"What type is that?"

"The love-'em-and-leave-'em type. The, I-want-you-so-bad-right-now-but-tomorrow-I-won't-remember-your name type. So let's forget this conversation and have a good time for Carly's sake."

"I was trying to have a good time, sugar," Ty pressed on, studying her face as if he was trying to get a deeper read on her. "You're a tough one, aren't you?"

"Just because I didn't fall for your lines doesn't make me all that tough." Especially as she'd been ready to succumb to his more-than-impressive charms.

Idiot.

She turned her back on him and threaded her way through the crowd, stopping to politely tell a man named Tiny, who had to be well over three hundred pounds, that she didn't need another drink and, no, she didn't want to dance.

Ty caught up to her when she was almost out the door. "Where are you going?"

"Just tell Carly I had to leave, okay? Make sure Hunt gets her home."

"You didn't want to dance with Tiny?" he asked.

"Not especially."

"He thinks you're awfully cute." He looked at her with those not-so-innocent eyes, and there was half an apology in his tone when he spoke next. "And so do I."

"I already told you—"

"That you're not into bad boys," he finished. "But Samantha, I can be very good."

"You're impossible."

"And it took you a whole ten minutes to catch on to that? I'm definitely losing my touch."

"I'm out of here before this goes any further." Still, she couldn't bring herself to take another step out the door. Despite his blatant come-ons, there was something appealing about his confidence. The way the come-on might've actually been more tongue in cheek than anything else. A way to get her to react, perhaps? It appealed to her wild, erotic fantasy-writing side.

"Look, if you stay, I'll try and behave," he said.

She knew full-well he had no intention of behaving. By the look he gave her, he knew she knew it, too. She offered him a small smile and let him lead her to one of the tables along the far wall.

"We'll start over," Ty suggested. "And I won't flirt with you. Much." He motioned to the waitress, and within a few minutes of casual small talk about the weather, they had more beers.

She leaned forward on her elbows, guessing how long he'd be able to control himself, and wished she didn't want him to. "So, what do you do?"

"Like, for a living?" he teased.

"We could start there," she said.

He shrugged. "I do a little bit of everything. Bartend, bounce. I was a bounty hunter for a while, auto mechanic, rebuilt classic Harleys, repo man, wrestled alligators for fun and profit…"

"So basically, all the dangerous jobs this side of the military," she said.

"I guess between Jon and me, we've got all the bases covered." He paused, saw the confusion on her face. "Hunt's real name is Jonathan. I never could get used to calling him by that nickname."

"Do you guys get together often?"

"With my travels and his, these visits are few and far between. It's been good to see him again." He crossed a long leg, ankle over knee, and balanced his beer bottle on his thigh.

"How long are you in town?" she asked.

"Maybe a week. Then I head back out."

"To where?"

He shrugged and grinned. "I don't have a plan. I just go and things tend to fall into place."

"Isn't that scary?" Did she sound ridiculous asking a man who did the things he'd named for a living if he was frightened of not having his life mapped out? But he answered her seriously, without a hint of that bravado she'd witnessed earlier.

"Yeah, sometimes it is. Sometimes, though, fear feels right." He took a pull from his beer. "So, you and surfer girl been friends long?"

"Since college."

"Do you surf?"

She laughed. "The closest I get to surfing is watching it from the shore. She offered to teach me, but I'd rather catch a tan than catch a wave."

"You seem like you wouldn't have a problem handling yourself in the water. Or anyplace."

"I'm not like Carly," Sam said. "I'm not adventurous. I like stability. A roof over my head. A way to pay my bills."

She didn't bother to tell him that she'd grown up without any of those things, since she wasn't bitter. Not really. She'd made her peace with her mother and she'd moved on. However, her mother's wanderlust was in Sam's blood, beating underneath the surface. She'd had to try her hardest when she felt the urge to pick up and follow Carly while she was still on the pro surfing tour. But Sam's practicalness stopped her, even though she knew Carly would've helped her along, given her a place to stay if she'd needed one.

"But you have had that urge to pick up and leave it all behind, haven't you?"

"What makes you think that?"

Now it was his turn to lean forward on the table. His direct gaze made her cheeks heat. It was as if he could see straight through her. "It's in your eyes. I've seen it in my own," he said.

"You've known me for all of half an hour and you think you know everything, don't you?"

"I think you just answered my question. Keep in mind that being practical's not always the best way to live."

Her practicalness struggled to keep control, especially because Ty was talking freedom and the open road, and she could only concentrate on his mouth and how good his lips would probably feel on hers. She was thinking she probably wouldn't have to spice up her sex life if she was having sex with Ty.

For a moment, she imagined what would happen if she shifted into his lap, into her very own call to adventure. She took several sips of beer instead and remembered that this was supposed to be Carly's adventure, not hers.

She was ordering water on the next round.

"What are you thinking about, Samantha?"

"I'm thinking that I'm good at reading people, too."

"So read me." Ty sat back again.

She hesitated for a minute because she figured this one was too easy. But he'd asked for it. Even though she was beginning to more than enjoy his company, reminding him that she was onto him, and maybe even bringing him down a peg or two, wasn't a bad idea.

"You're a loner," she said.

"Yeah, pretty much," he agreed. "What else?"

"We already know that you're into one-night stands. So you're not into relationships, you're commitment phobic and probably scared to death of growing up," she explained.

He watched her, not noticeably uncomfortable with anything she said, but she had to have hit a nerve. The man was walking sex, personified. A never-settle-down, ride-off-into-the-night-on-his-bike type, who'd probably take better care of his Harley than a woman. Well, out of bed, anyway. Because the way his long fingers slowly traced the arms of the chair made her squirm in her seat.

She pulled herself back to reality. "How am I doing?"

"You seem pretty sure of yourself so far."

"I think my assessment's good. Unless you've got some kind of secret life no one knows about."

"Are you asking me or telling me?" he joked.

She caught the subtle shift he made in his chair, the way his eyes averted hers for a millisecond.

Her students didn't call her the human lie detector for nothing. But she hadn't expected Mr. Let It All Hang Out to confirm anything that easily.

"I'm telling you," she replied.

"You've got to improve your people-reading skills," he said. "Need another beer?"

"No, I'm..." she started, but he was already walking to the bar and he wasn't looking back. She got up and followed him, then spotted Carly and Hunt on the dance floor.

What they were doing wasn't technically dancing, but she didn't have time to think about that. She caught up with Ty at the bar, and tapped on his arm until he faced her. Although he smiled, she knew he wasn't happy.

"I've upset you," she said, and was shocked when he didn't deny it. Ty was a hundred percent bad boy but she suddenly had the feeling that this bad boy had much more of a sensitive side than anyone knew.

Without thinking, her hand went to the back of his

neck, and she pulled him down toward her. A quick kiss deepened when he put his arms around her waist, and she didn't protest until he broke away.

She pulled him back down for more.

TY KNEW HE SHOULD'VE LET Samantha leave the bar—and him—earlier. Because now that he'd tasted her, not tasting her would be hard.

"Let me get this straight," he said. "You're mad when I come onto you, but it's okay when you jump me?" he asked when he'd finally forced himself to end her kiss. Still, his mouth stayed poised only inches above hers.

"I wouldn't exactly call this jumping you, but yes."

"I'll never understand women," he muttered, releasing her. "Look, you were right before when you said I was only after one thing. Let's leave it then and I'll search for that one thing, since I'm sure I can find it here."

The ultimate cosmic joke—to now find a woman he felt that immediate connection with, which he'd always wanted.

He was losing something, all right, but it wasn't his touch. There was something about Samantha, something so fresh, so new, so...

She was freakin' adorable.

She doesn't want a one-night stand with you, Ty.

And what is it you want, again? Because it sure as hell wasn't to reveal his secrets to a total stranger when he couldn't even tell his own family.

"Ty." She touched his shoulder. "Secrets are okay for tonight."

She pushed him back onto the stool and made herself comfortable by positioning herself between his legs, and he realized that the entire bar had gone a bit more than rowdy.

Hell yeah, secrets were going to be more than okay tonight.

"Now it's my turn to read you, Samantha."

Undeterred, he gently took her arms and wrapped them around his waist.

"Okay. Go ahead."

"You want to be a little wild."

"I told you I'm not wild," she protested, but he knew better because Samantha kissed unlike any of the wild women he'd ever known and hell, he'd known a lot.

"Maybe it's time you let loose. Let yourself go and see where it takes you. Unless you're scared." He traced a perfect bottom lip with his finger, thought about how, with his next kiss, he was going to tug it gently between his teeth.

"Is this some kind of dare?"

"No dare. Just an offer."

"What kind of offer?"

"I'll tell you after I kiss you for a while longer," he said, then put his hands on her hips and pulled her closer to him, close enough so she could feel the kind of offer he planned on making her. There was no way any other woman was going to satisfy him tonight, and though he was torn about sending her away, he swore to himself that he wasn't going to hurt her.

She knows what she's getting into.

"I'd never kissed someone with a tattoo before," she said finally.

"Yeah? How'd you like it?"

She smiled, a wide, beautiful smile that hit him hard. "I think you'll have to refresh my memory."

This time, she didn't protest when he covered her mouth with his.

12

HUNT HAD GONE FROM kissing Carly to fighting off a group of men intent on damaging Cash, all in the space of a minute.

His fist connected with a cheekbone at the same time someone tried to put his kidneys out with a chair swiped from the outside patio. He swung around and took the guy out, and Cash came up behind him and saved him from another blow.

"Damn, that's going to hurt tomorrow." Hunt stared at his fist, which threatened to turn black and blue. His knuckles were already raw.

"Tell me about it. A guy can't even get some innocent companionship around this place," Cash complained. He had a small cut above his right eyebrow, but other than that, he'd fared well. Both of them had, against a crowd that should've been big enough to take them both down in minutes flat. A crowd led by the boyfriend of the red-headed woman, who'd conveniently forgotten to mention to Cash that she was indeed taken.

That was par for the course for Cash, and one of the major reasons he told everyone and anyone who listened that he never planned on walking the line for any damned woman alive. None of them were faithful, he'd say, so why the hell should he even pretend to make that promise? He liked to blame his attitude on his mother's fondness for

Johnny Cash and a curse that seemed to follow Cash no matter where he went. Hunt had to admit his friend had the worst luck in that department.

"Maybe next time, you could ask if she's got a boyfriend first. Like, before your pants are down," Hunt suggested.

"Not a bad idea, man. I'll take it under advisement. But this place did need livening up and I figured you'd be up for it."

Hunt just shook his head. The bouncers hadn't been any help, since they'd only just arrived to corral the last of the men, who'd had their asses handed to them.

Ty was the reason he and Cash didn't get kicked out with the rest of the group. Not that Ty had bothered to tear his goddamned lips away from Samantha's until Hunt had given Carly a push in Ty's direction with a look of, *keep her safe.* Which was something that hadn't made Carly happy at all, although Hunt acknowledged nothing got his blood more primed and ready for sex than a good, old-fashioned bar fight.

"You're not going to do that at the wedding, are you?" Carly asked seriously when Hunt returned to the table, Cash in tow. "Because, as much as I want to shake things up with my parents, this wasn't what I had in mind."

"I didn't exactly start this," Hunt said.

"You're getting married? What the hell's wrong with you?" Cash asked.

"I'm not getting married," Hunt insisted more forcefully than necessary. Sam and Ty watched the show unfold, meanwhile Hunt was worried. He was already tired of being on stage as the on-demand boyfriend.

"Ever?" Carly asked at the same time Cash spoke.

"Damned right you're not. No offense, Carly," Cash

said to her. "I just don't trust women any farther than I can throw them."

"Which won't be very far if you don't get out of here. And now," Hunt told his friend, who nodded and backed away. Hunt lowered his voice. "And no, I don't see marriage in my future. Why? Are you bucking for a big society wedding like your sister's?"

"That's not what I meant." She bit her bottom lip. "I mean, I'm not against marriage. To the right person."

"Who's the right person?"

"I don't know."

"Then maybe you need to stop thinking about finding the right guy and let yourself feel. What did Candy Valentine call it? Something about over the falls?"

"That means losing control," Carly said.

He pulled her against him as she spoke, heard his voice roughen and saw the fire flash briefly behind her baby blues. "Aren't you ready to lose control yet?"

"I think one of us needs to stay in control. And since it's not you, or those two, I guess I'm the one."

"I didn't know Sam needed a chaperone."

"She doesn't. But your brother does."

Hunt wasn't sure whether he should have explained what Ty was like, but when he'd been dancing with Carly earlier, his brother had been the last thing on his mind. In fact, if she'd let him, he would've made a break with her for the beach, and let what was going to happen happen that much sooner.

"Come on, Shark-lady, and dance with me." Ty escorted Carly onto the dance floor before either she or Hunt could protest.

Sam stared after Ty for a second, a small smile playing on her lips.

"Looks like you two really got to know each other," Hunt said to Sam.

"He's pretty special. Once you get past the act."

"Sounds as if you've got him pegged, and trust me, that doesn't happen often. He's pretty crazy."

"That's funny, coming from someone like you."

"Touché." He clinked the neck of his beer bottle with hers. At least everyone was having a damned good time tonight. That's what his orders had been, straight from his CO: *Have a good time.*

He always followed orders. Well, most of the time. Otherwise, he just made sure he didn't get caught, which was why his CO had added, *and don't get yourself arrested.*

So far, Hunt was two for two. Now, if he could get Carly to lighten up, things would really improve.

"So did you go to a lot of Carly's competitions?" he asked, figuring it was time to try and get some information about her fear of the water. *Know your enemy* was his motto, but knowing your friend's enemy was equally important. Or your pretend girlfriend's.

Damn, this was weird, especially since there was no pretending when it came to how badly he wanted her.

"I mostly caught her local competitions," Sam answered. "But you want to know about the wipeout and her injuries."

"I've usually got a better poker face, but yeah, I do want to know more."

"It's probably not my place to tell you more."

"I know she retired when she got hurt."

"She told you that?"

He sighed. "I never could lie to a teacher."

"Well, you've got one right. She was planning on retiring, got hurt surfing one of her last competitions. Pipeline. It's a competition..."

"I know what Pipe is," he said quietly. "What were her injuries like?"

Sam gave him the run-down, and he fought to keep the emotions off his face, because how could a person live through something like that and still seem so strong?

"Look, I assumed she hadn't told you, but she mentioned the surfing lesson thing to me. I'm not sure she'll be able to keep that promise to you, Hunt. And if you're not going to be able to help her, better she knows it now."

Sam was asking if he would bail on the wedding, and run off on her friend. All he'd wanted was a week's leave. Instead, he'd gotten a fantasy that blew his mind and a woman to match.

He hated it when his personal life got complicated. This time, he had no one to blame but himself, although Ty was a close target, a lightening rod that seemed to draw trouble. Carly was fun trouble, but trouble to be sure, and he did not belong in her world, even if she wanted out of it.

"Sam, look," he started, but she held up her hand as though she knew what he was going to say.

"She won't fall apart if you don't go to the wedding. But I can't promise the same if you try to force her into the water." She paused. "I've known Carly for nine years, and I've never seen her scared of anything. Not like this."

"She hasn't been in the water since?"

Sam gauged how much more to tell him, and then leaned forward and whispered, "she hasn't been anywhere near it. I was shocked when she bought the house on the beach, I'm hoping it will help. But it won't happen before next week."

"What's next week?"

She shook her head. "I've revealed too many of Carly's secrets tonight. You want more, you'll have to get it straight from the source."

He wanted more all right. Problem was, he couldn't come to terms with how much more he wanted, and why. Nothing beyond wanting to help, he told himself.

"WHAT THE HELL ARE YOU doing to my brother?"

Carly stared at Ty, open-mouthed. His words were not friendly, but he continued to smile and move her around the dance floor.

"What am *I* doing? What do you think you're doing with your tongue down my best friend's throat?" She kept the smile plastered on her face as well, because two could play at this game.

"I'm not forcing her to be my pretend girlfriend, if that's what you're thinking. Why don't you hire an escort? At least he'll get paid for helping you." Ty smirked and she wondered what her friend could possibly see in him. He was obnoxious. Rude, even. Handsome, too, but that was beside the point.

"Hunt offered. And I'm not going to hurt him. He's simply attending a wedding with me, not marrying me. And I swear, if you hurt my friend…"

"Come on, Ty, share the wealth." A man who was almost as wide as he was tall was trying his best to pry her away from Ty. She hung on to Ty's arm for dear life, even though she wanted to wring his neck for taking advantage of Samantha.

Ty didn't let go of her, one arm firmly wrapped around her waist. He used the other to draw the guy close, using the front of his T-shirt to hold him trussed. "Unless you want to get seriously hurt, I suggest that you back the hell off. If you don't, I'll meet you outside and teach you some manners."

The man held his hands up and Ty let him go with a slight backward push against his chest. He stumbled and then disappeared into the crowd.

"You were saying?" Ty asked.

"Do you get into a lot of fights?"

"Do you ask a lot of strange men to family weddings?"

"What are you expecting to happen with my friend?" she asked, hand on Ty's chest, because she was done fooling around now.

"We're having fun."

"Too much fun," she said and stopped dancing. "She's not thinking clearly."

"I'm not going to kidnap her, Carly. She'll have plenty of time to decide on her own if she wants to come with me when I leave."

What was he talking about?

The music shut down and the bartender announced last call before she had a chance to ask Ty. Hunt's brother walked her back to the table, where she motioned for Sam to follow her, which Sam did, after Ty gave her a lingering kiss. A kiss that left Sam giddy enough to actually giggle as she and Carly waited in the women's bathroom line.

"We need to get you home," Carly told her.

"I'm going home with Ty," Sam said. "And then, I'm going with him on his next road trip."

"He mentioned something about that."

"He's decided on Vegas, and he invited me along."

"I don't think that's the best idea."

"I think it's the best idea I've had in a long, long time," Sam said, giggling again.

It occurred to Carly that she'd never seen her friend this happy or relaxed.

"This must be how you felt, all the time, when you were riding the waves or stirring up trouble."

There was a tug in her gut at the truth of Sam's words. She had met a lot of people on her travels, but she hadn't kept many friends, or even acquaintances, from those days. Most of them had managed to fall away with the same speed as the waves.

Speaking of careers and surfing, what was she thinking? The event was next week, her sister's wedding right after and she wasn't prepared for either. "Why don't we get a cab home and you can sleep this off?"

"I might get a tattoo."

"Good thing they don't tattoo drunk people anymore."

"I'm not drunk, Carly. I've had two beers. And Ty said he could do it himself."

Perfect. Just perfect. "I'll bet he can. Probably learned it in prison or something."

"He's never been to prison. I mean, at least I don't think so."

"All I'm saying is that you don't know much about him, and you're going to just hop on the back of his bike and leave? That's not like you."

"Maybe it is." Sam's earlier giddiness suddenly dissipated, and Carly knew that her friend was high on Ty and nothing else. That made the situation even more dangerous.

"Do you have a secret life I don't know about?"

"Just because I had trouble writing my own fantasy doesn't mean that I don't have them," Sam explained. "And he fulfills all my requirements."

All the requirements Sam had spent her adult life insisting that she didn't want in a guy. No wild men, no commitment-shy bad boys. Ty fit both bills at first glance and beyond.

13

BY THE TIME CARLY AND SAM had gotten in and out of the bathroom, the bar was closing, and they followed the crowd outside. Hunt and Ty were standing by their bikes waiting for them, and Sam immediately left her side and went toward Ty. Carly marched up to Hunt because maybe he could bring some common logic to this equation. She stopped next to him.

"What's up?" Hunt asked.

"Your brother, that's what. He invited Sam to ride with him to Vegas. And she told him she'd go."

"It's not like he's leaving tonight."

"Do you see what you've done? You've disrupted everything."

"From what I've heard, that was the way you used to like things," he said. She made a mental note to kill her best friend, once she got her away from Ty's clutches.

Carly knew she'd started all this with her spice-up-your-sex life, Candy Valentine erotic writing. But from the looks of it Sam would be the one to finish it. From the way she was kissing Ty, it was obvious that there was no need for fantasy writing. There was enough steam coming off them to spark a fire.

Anger ran through Carly just as hot, but was quickly replaced by defeat and finally, sadness. Things were falling apart, people were raising hell and Hunt was right. There was a time, not all that long ago, when she would have been right in the middle of things. A time she would've beaten Hunt to the water for a naked swim and been the one to suggest an impromptu road trip to Vegas.

There was a time when she'd done things differently, shaken things up even when they'd been shaken. Instead, her enormously shy best friend was ready to hop on a motorcycle and take off cross-country, and she herself was ready to give up.

Carly'd already admitted defeat when she'd stopped getting on that board. There was no turning back. "I can't let her go."

"He's not going to take advantage of her," Hunt said solemnly, and she caught the defensiveness in his voice.

"She's had too much to drink," she lied.

"She's having fun and she's all grown up."

"She has responsibilities. A job. She can't quit and drop all this."

"You did."

She had. Took off at eighteen and headed to Pipe on spring break and never looked back. Not really. "That's not the same," she protested. "And you don't know anything about me."

"I know a lot more than you think."

"I'm not looking for someone to know me. This talk about weddings has you confused. I'm not looking for a commitment or a relationship, or a shrink, so if that's what you're looking for—"

"I'm looking for pleasure," he interrupted her. "Not any sort of commitment. Never wanted one of those, at least not outside my job. I'm not looking for anything but fun. A little bit of fantasy." He stood. "I'll take you home."

"Don't bother. I can catch a cab."

"I'm not going to run after you, so I hope you're not expecting that."

Her throat tightened, she looked over at Ty and Samantha and her anger fizzled. The next words she said were from that bold place, from the strong woman who'd taken on waves that had reduced bigger people to their knees.

Carly was through being scared, at least about certain needs. "I'm expecting you in my bed tonight. And anywhere else I want you," she said before grabbing him by the sleeve of his T-shirt and bringing him toward her. He didn't resist, in fact, and he kissed her back with a need that rivaled her own.

"So you're ready?" Hunt asked when she stepped away. Sam was already climbing onto Ty's motorcycle, and Carly accepted the helmet Hunt handed her, not bothering to ask why he wasn't going to wear one.

He was hard-headed enough already.

When she was secure on the seat behind him he gunned the motor, leaving her no choice but to wrap her arms around him as he headed the bike up the ramp of the freeway.

All that power, and Hunt, positioned firmly between her legs. The wind blew in her face, and the force of the loud engine reverberated along every square inch of skin. Her fantasy kicked up to a new level. She knew the SEAL had some wicked plans for her.

Well, she had some for him, too. He'd been right about sooner than later, and about losing control. At least for the night.

She wondered how Nicole would take it if they rode up to the church on this bike, since Carly had just acquired a newfound fondness for Harleys.

WHEN THE RIDE UP THE coast toward Samantha's place didn't make Ty feel any better, he knew he was in for it. He just wasn't sure how into it he was prepared to get. To top it off, Jon would be majorly pissed about this, if surfer girl hadn't been even more so. He owed Jon a big thank you for being so focused on taking surfer girl home, and to bed. Then he asked himself if he wouldn't have been better off sending Samantha home on her own.

He wasn't a guy anyone would accuse of being a romantic soul unless they knew him well. Few did, considering he didn't stick around in any one place, but if and when the time came, he'd always planned on settling down.

Wasn't it a bitch that he'd found that woman when he could only offer her unsettled.

And he'd known, dammit, the second he'd talked with Samantha, the second she'd called him on his behavior and then asked him about his secrets.

Ty stopped brooding when he pulled up to Samantha's apartment, pushed the bike into Neutral and helped her off the back. When she took the helmet off, her dark hair tumbled out onto her shoulders.

"What did you think of the ride?" he asked.

"I loved it."

"Most bike virgins do," he said.

She stopped smiling. "I guess you've had your share of bike virgins, then."

"A few," he said softly. "Look, maybe I should go." He understood that the rush of feeling in the bar, with the pounding music and alcohol and the anything-goes atmosphere was disappearing quickly.

She shook her head. "No. It's okay. I might be slightly sensitive tonight. My boyfriend and I just broke up," she said. "Honestly, he broke up with me."

"His loss."

"He wouldn't agree."

"Then he doesn't deserve you. What was his problem?"

She hesitated for a second. "He said I was too forward. Sexually."

"That would never be a problem for me," he said, and saw her shift uneasily. He put a hand under her chin and forced her to meet his eyes. "I like you the way you are."

"I'm not very experienced," she said. And she didn't blush or hide away. "But I know what I like."

"And I'm going to make sure there's an awful lot you'll like tonight." He slid the strap of her tank top off one shoulder and kissed it.

"I may have been a bike virgin, but I think I'll surprise you."

"Baby, you already have," he whispered against her ear.

"Go slow, Ty," she whispered back. Once he walked her inside her apartment and she locked the door behind them, he sat her next to him on the couch and kissed her. He kissed her until she was breathing hard, clutching at his back, and he pulled away to make sure that yes, she was okay with this. So okay that she'd moved onto his lap.

Her lips were swollen from the kisses, and he ran the pad of his thumb over her bottom lip while his other hand traveled down her lower back to cup her ass.

"So what happened with the boyfriend to scare him off?" Ty asked, because he had to know more about Samantha. Somehow, he didn't ever see her turning a man off.

"I wrote him about what I wanted," she paused, "in bed. My fantasy."

"Do you still have the paper?" he asked.

"Why?"

"I want to read it," he replied. He wanted to make this night special for her, wanted to replace the memory of her jerk ex-boyfriend's reaction to her fantasy with one that could make her smile.

She moved out of his arms reluctantly and then grabbed his hand so he would follow her into her bedroom. She riffled through a dresser drawer and brought out a folded paper, and handed it to him tentatively.

Ty took it, sat back on her bed, propped his head on his arm and began to read. Sam left the room. But not long after he came up behind her in the kitchen, took a glass of water from her hand and put his arms around her. He'd taken off his shirt and instinctively she ran her hands along his chest and his shoulders, and he smiled that lazy smile he'd first given her in the bar.

"So, what did you think?" she asked.

"I think we'll have to act out every single detail of that fantasy," he said. "But first, you're going to have to do one more thing for me."

"What's that?"

"Read it for me. To me. Out loud."

"Ty, I can't…"

"Yeah, you can. Trust me," he whispered, then started to lead her to the bedroom.

"Wait. Now you know some of my secrets," she said. "So isn't it only fair you share some of yours?"

She ran a hand down his arm, over the tribal tattoo that circled his bicep, and he felt the instant connection with her touch.

"You don't want to know the half of it," he said.

"Then tell me half of it."

He almost didn't, urged himself to hold back completely—the way he always had because it was easier not to speak about it or think about it. But it wasn't going away, no matter how hard he tried, and he couldn't bring himself to tell Jon. Not yet.

"Tell me," she said again, right before she stood on her tiptoes and put her mouth on his, with such ease that he crumbled.

To be fair, he'd crumbled earlier when she'd seen right through his act.

Hours before, she'd been telling him off and now she was his.

"One secret," she murmured against his mouth

"I think you're so right for me that it hurts."

She smiled in a way that told him she hadn't had as much to drink as he'd thought, that she was here because she wanted to be, not because of beer-goggles or an ex-boyfriend or a rebound.

"Tell me more," she urged.

"Not tonight, Samantha. I'll tell you everything in the morning." He looked her in the eye and waited for her reaction.

When she tugged him close again, he knew that everything was somehow going to be okay. He didn't want to question it further. Tonight, he would find some peace in Samantha's willing arms.

14

THROWN OVER HUNT'S shoulder, his arm securely around her waist, Carly was ready to give the term *sex on the beach* her own special meaning.

Something, everything about the caveman style move he used was more of a turn-on than she'd ever had. And when he set her down by the dunes behind her lanai, hidden by palm trees, her breath was already fast.

"What do you want?" he asked, his eyes heavy-lidded with the same lust she'd seen on the dance floor. Except he wasn't going to wait the way he had on the dance floor.

"I want to be able to let go and not worry about anything else."

"Were you thinking about other things last night?"

"I was thinking that I wanted more," she whispered while his hand traveled under her shirt, along her stomach and skirted down to the button on her jeans.

"Me, too. A lot more."

She pressed her lips against the base of his throat, and the rumble of his suppressed groan vibrated against her mouth while he pulled her jeans down. She kicked out of them and he didn't bother with her top when he put his hands on her hips, picked her up and carried her to the large palm tree that backed up to the dune.

She didn't stop kissing him. Her hands firmly around

his shoulders, her tongue teasing his, he pushed back and sank to his knees on the sand in front of her.

So this is what it takes to bring a warrior to his knees.

She watched him watch her and took a long, hitched breath. He was waiting for her to make the next move and part of her wanted to let him lay her down on the sand and take over. But this was her show. No turning away now.

"Take these off," she said finally, brushing her thumbs against the bands of lace riding low on her hips. Carly could barely hear her own voice.

The way he looked at her, she'd never felt more desired in her life, or more desirable. She wasn't broken or scared and she wanted Hunt, all of him and any way she could get him.

She wanted to finish this fantasy.

Impatiently, he whisked off the slip of fabric and waited for her direction.

"Hunt, please," she said, not sure if she would be able to get the words out. "I want…"

She stopped, guided his head toward her and he let her off the hook, dipped his face into the blond triangle at the juncture of her thighs and she moaned.

Her hands tightened in his hair as he held her hips and spread her legs apart. She leaned against the trunk of the old palm, the bark biting the skin between her shoulder blades. She didn't care about that, or that she was exposed to the night air and to Hunt, who looked up at her one final time before kissing her, right between her legs. His tongue found her sweet spot, kissed and licked until she was pulsing with need. She arched away from the tree, pushing herself into his hands and his mouth.

He urged one of her legs over his shoulder, allowing him more access to her and the frenzy shivered through her. The leg still on the ground trembled, the other spreading her wider, and his tongue took full advantage. Right about there she knew she'd lost the power of coherent speech because it was random moans and sighs and *more, Hunt, please more, more, more.* The sensations rose up and filled her as his tongue danced around her clit.

And then she was coming, hard against his mouth, hips pressing wantonly forward as he continued to tongue her, not easing up at all. His fingers bit into the soft flesh of her thighs. Everything on her body was more sensitive than it had ever been, and just when she thought she couldn't stand it any longer, one orgasm rolled seamlessly into a second.

When the night breeze fluttered by her, she became vaguely aware of Hunt disengaging and holding her steady against the trunk of the tree.

"Did you ever do that before, like that, with anyone?" he murmured against her neck.

"No…never…"

"Good. I like being first. And this night is far from over." With that, his hands skimmed her shirt up over her breasts, urging her out of it.

By the time she'd lowered her arms, he'd already flicked his tongue over one nipple. She sucked in a quick breath when his mouth left it and the cooler air met the wet and made her nipple taut. He did the same with her other nipple and she tried to force his head back down to one of them. He resisted and she groaned in frustration.

And then he smiled, caught her wrists easily in one of his hands and extended them over her head. His was a wicked, wicked grin that made her body pulse and she knew what he planned to do.

She was really giving up control now, and he watched

her carefully, waiting for her to nod her assent. When she did, he reached down and grabbed his discarded T-shirt and bound her wrists together, then held them above her head.

His mouth was on her breast again, his hand between her legs, stroking her. She arched up to meet him, alternately tugging on her restraints and remembering she couldn't stop him if she wanted to.

She didn't want him to, not at all. The skin on his cheeks and chin was rough against hers and she liked that, too.

Carly heard him tug his zipper, smiled when she saw the tuft of hair and realized going commando was a way of life for him. He yanked the jeans down over his ass, left them down around his ankles and rolled on a condom with his free hand.

She wrapped a leg around him and he was inside her that fast. Fast and hard and standing were becoming her new favorite ways to have sex. "Oh, yeah, that's it."

She had no quarter and didn't want it, moved her other leg up and locked both around his back. He shifted and pushed deep inside of her. Together they rocked until she was coming again, contracting around him.

"Come with me, Hunt," she murmured, although it came out more like a command. He groaned and began to pulse inside her.

IT WAS A RUSH BEING WITH a woman who was in prime athletic condition and whose drive matched his. And, since Carly's hands weren't free, she used every available muscle to force him to force her to lose control.

Come with me, Hunt….

He held her wrists firmly against the palm tree as its

leaves swayed and rustled in the light wind. Cushioning her lower back with his free hand, he drove into her until he couldn't stand it another second and let himself come with a loud cry.

Mind-blowing.

That's all he kept repeating to himself over and over as he closed his eyes and recovered. He let go of her arms and she eased them around his shoulders, although he hadn't untied her wrists yet. Her body stuck to his. The two of them both damp with sweat from exertion, the kind that left you feeling as if you'd conquered the biggest roller coaster and still wanted to go for another ride.

There wasn't a feeling in the world comparable to this. Jumping out of a plane into a mission came close, but it was a different kind of heart-pounding, adrenaline-filled rush. This one lingered in his bones, left his muscles quivering and left a beautiful, naked woman pressed against his chest.

This was far beyond any fantasy.

"MMMM, LET'S STAY OUT here," Carly said when he picked her up again, yet she really, really liked it when he picked her up and put her exactly where he wanted her.

"Don't want surfer girl getting swept up by the thunderstorm," he told her.

She opened her eyes and looked at the rapidly swirling wind and the lightening-filled sky. She heard the ocean surf pounding against the beach, and felt the first heavy raindrops hit her bare skin.

The electricity blinked off, then on, once they were inside the house, and she tried to think candles and flashlights before realizing she didn't care about any of that.

She just wanted Hunt to keep his arms around her, to keep doing what he did so well.

Candy Valentine certainly had the right idea. That woman deserved a raise. And she'd write to *Total Woman Magazine* and tell them that, as soon as she had another orgasm or two.

He carried her up the stairs with no effort and when he laid her down on her bed, she pulled at his shoulders.

"Don't leave," she said.

"Are you sure?"

"The fantasy doesn't end with you leaving," she said.

"I didn't realize *I* was in the actual fantasy."

"You are now. Too far in for you to go."

"You're shivering. And wet," he said, but his hand wasn't reaching for any kind of towel.

She grinned, shifted and pulled the covers over both of them, and the lights came up again. He dimmed her lamp and glanced out the window.

"It's a bad one," she murmured.

"It's nothing," he said. "If it was going to turn into anything, I'd have been called back in." This wasn't a hurricane, or even a tropical storm because when either hit the Eastern Seaboard, every military person in sight was utilized. And he could think of many other ways he'd like to be utilized tonight.

Carly had closed her eyes, her breathing deep and even.

He planned on letting her nap and waking her up better than an alarm clock ever could. His hand stroked her thigh lightly, felt for the scar he knew was there. Her eyes opened, but she didn't seem self conscious, didn't turn away from his touch.

"Your surgeon was good," Hunt said. He lifted the covers and ran a finger along the faintly pink scar on the outside of her right thigh. And then he touched the other scar, the longer one he'd felt along her spine for the first time tonight.

For a lot of women, the scars would've been the bigger blow, but Carly wasn't most women. As an athlete, Hunt knew she saw her body as a tool to get her where she needed to go. Her self-confidence in that sense showed, despite the fact that she was experiencing a temporary setback in the surfing department.

"Only the best for the Winters' women," she said. "The best high society has to offer. And you have a nice collection yourself."

"Wear them with pride, I always say." He pointed to the nearly invisible scar on his side. "This is my most recent. The enemy decided I shouldn't stop him from escaping."

"I'm glad he didn't succeed in stopping you."

"Yeah, me too." He paused. "Want to tell me about your scars?"

"I don't want to talk about work," she said.

"What do you want to talk about, then?"

"I don't plan on either of us doing too much talking right now," she said, reaching down between his legs.

Oh, yeah, he could live with that.

He was already heavy and hard against her palm, and he rolled onto his back and let her stroke him for a few minutes. She leaned in, her breasts brushing his chest and she kissed him, then caught his lower lip between her teeth and sucked gently.

He tucked one of his arms under his head while she kissed him, letting his free hand roam over her bare back. She continued stroking him with one hand, let her other move lower between his legs and smiled against his mouth when he moaned.

"You're a bad, bad girl, Carly Winters," he murmured when she let him up for air.

"What? You think I'm corrupting you?" she asked as her fingertips continued to tease probably the most sensitive area on his body next to his cock. His hips rose off the bed.

"Yeah, I do," he managed to choke out, sure he was losing brain cells to her touch by the second.

Carly's thumb circled the ring of muscle around the head of his cock as she nipped his earlobe. Then she licked along the outer ridge of his ear and down his neck, murmuring, "put it in my file, right next to that fax."

"You're in so much trouble."

"I'm shaking," she said, her teeth capturing one of his nipples, the sensation a direct hit to his groin.

His balls tightened, he heard his own breath grow ragged and finally, he called uncle. "Not like this, baby. I want to be inside you when I come. Please."

She nipped his neck as she acquiesced, moved her hands away slowly and the sensations lingered on his skin. It was her turn to lie back on the tangled sheets, looking so damned sexy with a deep flush coloring her cheeks and her breasts. He stopped everything so he could stare at her for a few seconds. He let her fingers trace her nipples, dark pink and taut and she met his gaze. Her lips parted and he knew she was ready.

Hunt urged her onto her side so she faced away from him and toward the uncovered window that the rain continued to sluice against mercilessly. He discovered that he'd been right about his tattoo theory. Carly hadn't stopped at one.

He traced a delicate line of three small dolphins, outlined in a very light gray and filled in with an even lighter shade of blue-gray, in mid-jump from a series of waves. The whole thing was maybe three inches in length and unobtrusive—almost invisible to anyone who wasn't looking for it and placed low enough to be covered when she wore a bikini.

This one was personal.

"I got that after the accident," she whispered.

"It's beautiful. Just like you, Carly," he said. He pushed his chest against her back. His hand skimmed her smooth stomach until his fingers dipped toward her sex and his face nuzzled against her shoulder.

The storm shook the house.

Carly was wet for him and he kept her legs spread with his thigh while he teased her. Eventually her thighs shook from the strain and she begged for him.

She rolled so she was on her stomach, pushed up onto her hands and knees and he covered her with his body, eased inside her and then helped her kneel up. His chest pressed her back as he held her hips in place and thrust into her. She put her hands against the headboard for support while he took her, her heat so welcoming that he buried himself to the hilt and she whimpered with pleasure.

"Don't stop. Don't you dare stop, Hunt," she cried out.

"You're still in too much trouble to give orders," he said, and it was trouble she never wanted to be rid of, the best kind. It was going to leave her legs too weak to walk, the kind that made her abs clench and her moans throaty and constant and almost as loud as his.

Sex had never been this good. Ever. She'd known, on some level, that it could be. That it should be. But this was as if her body finally got its act together and demanded its fill, and as much as she didn't want this to end, she needed that release. Had to have it.

She pushed backward, forcing him to her rhythm because she wanted him louder, wanted the bed to shake with the same kind of force and fury that shook her house. He took her challenge, took her with a single-minded intensity she wanted so much more of. When his hand moved forward to stroke her clit in tandem with his motion, she closed her eyes, listened when he groaned, *now, baby, now,* and let the orgasm rip through her. And when he came seconds later, with several intense, hard thrusts, he was yelling her name into the darkness.

15

SUN HIGH OVERHEAD, wind in his hair and salt water dancing in the wake of his wave runner, Hunt gunned it through the chop. He took a narrow turn by the reef and headed out for another run, prepared to fling his towed passenger, board and all, into the waves at full speed.

"Tow me in right behind the next setup!"

Hunt barely heard the shouted directive over the roar of the ocean, and he obliged by directing the wave runner toward the pounding swells, felt the line of the towed surfer and board tighten behind him. The waves were breaking off the far side, where he'd practiced rock portage as a BUD/s training for the SEALs. The dangerous, but necessary practice of transferring from rubber raft to the sharp and slippery rocks during some of the most brutal surf was hard to master. Judging by the swells he saw today, he knew any training exercises would've been called off.

Some of the best surfing to be found here occurred a few miles from that spot, or at least the best spot to practice the kind of extreme surfing that Cash liked best.

Cash had grown up in Tanzania, learned to surf amidst the sharks and waves of Dar Es Salaam. His parents were doctors who traveled to third-world countries for years at a time to practice medicine.

His teammate and friend spoke nineteen tribal dialects, and the six main romance languages, including Catalan, and enough to get by in three others. And he could curse well in all of them, which was something that happened loudly and often. He'd surfed competitively for a bit when he was younger, joined the Navy at seventeen and entered BUD/s at nineteen, and was one of the few who had actually enjoyed surf passage. He was also able to get Hunt into more trouble than Ty ever did, and always on a moment's notice, as evidenced by the previous night's escapades.

Hunt felt the tug on the rope and slowed down. "You don't want to go out farther?" he shouted back, slowed, then turned to ask when Cash didn't paddle past him into the swell.

His teammate sat balanced on his board, staring at the ocean. He put up his arm and motioned as he told Hunt, "the swell's maxed out. Not worth it."

He said this with a straight face, even as a ten-foot wave crashed against the rocks inland. It would've capsized the rubber raft. In these conditions, Cash had just declared it not extreme enough.

"What's getting thrown from one of those feel like?" Hunt asked, once they'd gotten to the dock leading to the Naval Base.

"It goddamned hurts."

"I'll bet it does," Hunt agreed, trying to picture Carly in waves like he'd seen today. Waves he knew were nothing compared to what she'd surfed.

"I didn't know you cared so much about me," Cash said. "I mean, why the sudden interest in surfing?" he asked, with a grin that indicated he knew exactly why Hunt was interested.

It was Hunt's luck that Cash had been with him and Carly last night, and subsequently knew the whole story about Hunt being the stand-in date. The evidence: Cash had started off the morning with, *I think what you're doing with surfer girl's a really bad idea.*

Hunt had started off the morning ignoring his friend.

Now, Cash shrugged. "I hadn't heard of her, but that doesn't mean anything. I follow a different side of the sport. And women don't get a lot of press, even a hot one like her," he explained. "You know, she and I would have a lot more in common if she wasn't looking for a boyfriend."

"Maybe you should keep your eyes off my hot surfer chick. Besides, she's not looking for any kind of commitment, and I think she's officially done with surfer dudes," Hunt said.

Cash held up his arms in surrender and mumbled something about how no one used the phrase *surfer dude* anymore. "And hey, you were the one who brought it up, remember?"

"She was hurt badly. As a result, she's afraid to go back in the water," Hunt admitted. "And if you tell her I told you, she'll kill me."

"I won't say a word. But it sounds like all she needs is a little bit of juju. You know, a good luck charm. Something that makes her think she's protected."

"I don't know if that's it. She seems so strong. Maybe she's just scared of being physically hurt again."

"That's not it. We've all been hurt bad, and I can guarantee that wasn't the first accident she had, even though it might've been the worst."

"So what now?" Hunt ran his hands through his hair in frustration.

"Whatever happened took away her confidence. And fear's a killer if it's not channeled," Cash replied.

For a second they were both silent. Hunt knew they

were thinking the same thing, about Hunt and Carly's time out, about how the two of them would put the fear to work for them, or else they wouldn't have a chance in hell of surviving.

"How do I do that?" Hunt asked.

"Slip her some juju. Although, judging by the way you were whistling this morning, you already did that," Cash said innocently, then took off down the dock as Hunt ran after him.

"ANY NEW TATTOOS I should know about?" Carly asked her friend through the cell phone's earpiece as she stood like a mannequin, on a raised pedestal, wearing the itchiest fabric known to man. Long abandoned by her mother and sister so Nicole could try on her wedding dress again, Carly got ahold of Samantha, who'd had her phone turned off for most of the morning.

"There might be. I tried my best to avoid all mirrors this morning before coming to school." Sam's voice sounded groggy, but there was a hint of something else in it, as well.

"Are you feeling that bad?" Carly was feeling really good after a ride up the coast that morning. The wind had been in her hair, the sun beating on her bare shoulders. Surprisingly, the feeling hadn't left her, even when she'd climbed into the bridesmaid's dress.

"I didn't get much sleep, so it's more a feeling that there's not going to be enough coffee in the world today. Ben, no headlocks in the hallway!" A pause, and then Sam spoke again. "Sorry, didn't mean to yell in your ear. Although I think my head just split in two."

"Well, it seemed you had a blast last night, and it obviously continued after then. When I didn't hear from you first thing this morning, I thought maybe you'd run off with Ty."

"One of us ran off, but it wasn't me," Sam said quietly. Carly cursed inwardly because she'd known this was going to happen. "Can I help?" she asked.

"I wish. But no, it's something I'll have to deal with on my own."

"That's something I understand all too well. But I'm here if you need me."

"Bell's ringing. I've got to run."

"We'll talk later," Carly promised, and clicked off. All she wanted to do was get out of the heels she'd stuffed her feet into and stretch.

She'd slept later than she had in ages, missed the dawn completely and woke firmly into Friday morning sun-up. Hunt wasn't in bed with her, but she could hear him. That was enough to cause her to move, although she was sore and ached in places she didn't remember ever aching in.

She'd liked that feeling. She had to try this stand-in boyfriend fantasy thing more often, especially with a man who was thoughtful enough to leave her notes that said, *see you for the dawn patrol tomorrow.*

Tomorrow, at dawn, she had plans to distract Hunt from his quest to surf. She'd make her stand-in help her play out her fantasy over and over again.

"Your boyfriend's going to love your cleavage."

Carly opened her mouth to tell the seamstress that she didn't have a boyfriend and caught her sister staring at her from the corner of the dressing room, eyebrows raised.

"What man wouldn't?" Carly answered, and really, the contraption she'd had strapped to her ribcage did give her cleavage, or at least, the illusion of it. However, breathing wasn't an option, but no one seemed to care about that.

She'd thought the fitting was one of the most painfully boring hours of her life, and that was compared to lying stock-still in a hospital bed, counting ceiling tiles. But then, she'd had prescription drugs to alter the pain. During the fitting, she'd had nothing as the seamstress spent the entire time painstakingly altering the bodice of the lime-green horror until it skimmed her upper body.

Carly'd been very wrong about the fitting being one of the worst, since she had lunch to endure.

"OH, GOOD, Marie got us a table," her mother said as they entered the restaurant.

Nicole continued to babble about how well her wedding dress fit now that she'd lost that pesky extra two pounds. Carly started to make a comment about ordering an extra dessert, but her mother's comment stopped her cold.

Marie. As in, Marie Tremont. As in… "Evan's mom, Marie?"

"Of course, dear. Did you forget she's one of my closest friends? And she hasn't seen you in ages."

Truth be told, half the time Carly hadn't even made it home for holidays—more often she'd been traveling and competing. *No time when you're training,* her coach always told her. Then came rehab.

Marie greeted Carly warmly, and the talk of the table centered around the wedding immediately, which seemed to let her off the hook. And from the way Nicole made it sound, she was having the event of the century. For all Carly knew, maybe she was.

None of Carly's friends, surfing or otherwise, had gotten married in any way, shape or form that rivaled Nicole's extravaganza-to-be. Carly had attended a few weddings on the beach, where bride, groom and guests were all happily barefoot and in bathing suits. The reception was always centered on riding out the late-afternoon tubes.

"Evan's not giving you up without a fight, you know," Marie said, and Carly stopped, mid-drink of her iced tea, and cursed herself for letting her guard, and her attention, wander.

"Well, he's going to have to," Carly replied. Corporate raider versus Navy SEAL. Could be interesting. The only advantage Evan had was that he might be able to bore Hunt to death.

"Carly, it's just that Evan has so much more to offer you than a military kind of life. I wish you'd give him a chance."

"Hunt does fine with what he offers me," she said, then heard the harshness in her voice and wondered why she was so upset. She was defending Hunt as if he was her boyfriend and not the guy who'd spent all of last night and most of the morning giving her orgasms worthy of a double close-out.

"Maybe Evan will have to rescue Carly from the waves, the way Hunt did," Nicole said.

"What are you talking about?" Carly asked, because she and Hunt certainly didn't have the chance to get their stories straight before, although she did remember him mentioning something. But he'd been kidding. At least, she'd thought so.

"That's the way Hunt told me you'd met when I asked him. The other day when I called and he picked up the phone," Nicole went on. "He said you were caught in a riptide, and even though you were clearly getting out of it on your own, he decided to rescue you anyway."

"He told you that?" Carly asked.

"He also said he made the decision when he saw that your top had come off and floated away," Nicole finished. Marie gasped.

"Evan wouldn't do anything like that," his mother said.

"No, Evan wouldn't," Carly agreed, then she smiled. The image of her topless in Hunt's arms would be enough to get her through the rest of the afternoon.

16

Sex was much, much better than physical therapy. Actually, it was the best thing her kitchen table, floor and counter had ever seen, and Carly wondered if she could get a doctor's prescription for it. Maybe she should stop complaining about Nicole's upcoming nuptials and start embracing them, because breaking in her date was the most fun she'd ever had.

"We're supposed to be practicing," she murmured, something she'd been telling Hunt for a couple of days. Under the guise of getting their story straight, they'd been spending an inordinate amount of time together. And while the sex could be deemed casual, and amazing, there were also dinners, phone calls, walks. Late-night movies. Teasing. Laughing. Enjoying.

Rather than "distracting" Hunt from wanting to learn to surf, she'd had to admit she was dating her pretend boyfriend. She also discovered that being with Hunt was like being pulled under a blue crush, and, for the first time, the idea of "way over her head" was very appealing.

She refused to think about how his leave was up sooner than later, and that he'd promised her absolutely nothing beyond the wedding. That was the way she wanted it, too, wasn't it?

He'd started kissing her shoulder, distracting her again.

They'd almost made it to the couch, but somehow ended up tangled on the rug halfway between the kitchen and living room, and in full view of the glass sliding doors, should anyone happen along there.

"Yes, practice," he said, and his hand slid up her inner thigh. He grinned when his fingers made contact because she was already wet for him. Again. "It's very important for me to know you. Inside and out."

He slid a finger inside her and she immediately contracted against his invasion. Then he slid in another, and when he added a third she arched against him and cried out.

"Just like I said, I'm getting to know all about you," he murmured while she wiggled against him, looking for relief from the slow ache building from his touch. "Getting to know all your secret spots."

Hunt's mouth brushed her collarbone and she moaned. His fingers twisted. His tongue circled her nipple lightly and the pad of his thumb circled her hot nub of flesh with just enough pressure to make her scream, which she did. Her yell was stifled because she bit down on his shoulder when she climaxed. He didn't seem to mind at all, murmured something about loving the way she looked when she came, against her ear.

"That's not exactly the kind of knowing that's going to get us through the wedding," she said, once she could speak again.

He rolled slightly away from her, lay flat on his back against the carpet and laughed, a deep, rich sound. "That's the kind of knowing that's going to get us through anything."

And when he stood, it was in one easy movement and she enjoyed her vantage point with him towering over her.

"And you've got to stop seducing me," Hunt told her, "or we'll miss the best surfing of the day. Again."

He'd come to the house before five in the morning. And come again a couple of times since then. Now, it was nearly six-fifteen and dawn was breaking.

Keeping his mind off surfing lessons and on her had worked for a while, but today, he seemed bound and determined not to let her off the hook. Time to think of a new plan.

"Come on, surfer girl. I'll make breakfast and then it's time for our first lesson." He hauled her to her feet and left her with a kiss so long and hot she thought maybe, just maybe, she'd changed his mind. But he did let her go and wandered off into the kitchen. She followed his broad, muscled figure as it retreated.

After a quick shower, Carly pulled on a bikini with boy-short bottoms out of habit because they were much more practical for surfing and ignored the sarcastic barb her own mind threw back at her for even thinking she was going near the water. Although she and Hunt had been spending a lot of time together in the evenings, their days were spent apart—he'd been with Ty, and she'd been busy with the magazine and with the charity event for spinal cord research. And since that night in the bar when Hunt learned about the accident, he hadn't pushed it.

This morning, she could tell he was going to push it. But maybe it would be different with Hunt there. Maybe she could get closer to the water, get her toes into the wet sand down by the shoreline. She felt the drive building up inside of her as she gazed out the window toward the waves. For the first time, Carly realized that she was equal parts excitement and fear. Not a bad start.

A smile on her face, she deleted the new phone message from Evan because she couldn't deal with that pressure anymore. The guy couldn't take a simple *no* for an answer, and he was a lot less persuasive than Hunt had been.

She found Hunt sitting on the lanai staring at the ocean. He wore only a pair of long swim trunks he must have had packed away in his Harley. He didn't turn when she slid the glass door open, just started talking instead.

"There's something special about dawn on the beach," he said.

Carly noticed that he sounded no different than any newly reformed or rabid surfer she encountered, including herself.

"I know what you mean." She sat next to him. "It's like it needs its own moment of silence."

"When I was in training for the SEALs, it was brutal. Beyond brutal. There were hours in there when I was sure I would die from exhaustion. There were times the pain was so bad I thought death would be the easiest option. And then I'd come up to like the thirty-sixth hour of no sleep and I'd look at the bell, since ringing out meant comfort. You rang out and you got a hot meal, a hot shower and sleep. And I'd tell myself, *hold out a few more minutes, Hunt. It's got to get better.* And then dawn would break and even the instructors left you alone for a few minutes, like sun-up hypnotized them, too."

He turned to face her. "No matter where I am in this world, this part of the day always makes things better."

"So, you're away a lot?" she asked, and he nodded. "That's got to be tough on relationships."

"Now you're worried about the love life of your fantasy boyfriend?"

Actually, it was something she'd been thinking about over the last few days, but hadn't wanted to bring up. Mainly, because she didn't want to know if he was a girl-at-every-port kind of guy. It shouldn't have mattered, but it did to her.

"Curious, not worried. I'm sure you have a fine love life," she said, but couldn't help casting a sideways glance to see if his expression would give anything away.

It didn't.

"If there were any girlfriends, I wouldn't be here with you. I told you, I'm not looking for more than a few nights in fantasyland, in general. Same as you."

"Oh." She rubbed her palms together, chose her next words carefully. "Have you ever?"

"Been the object of someone's fantasy? I thought I already was."

"Had a girlfriend? Been in love?"

"No to both. I never had the time or the inclination."

"Does your job keep you that busy, or are you like Cash?" she asked.

He lifted his eyebrows. "Like Cash?"

"You know, when he said he didn't trust women. Do you feel the same way?" she asked, and he stared off into the distance, as if he wasn't going to answer. When he didn't, she effectively had her answer.

"Want to talk about your love life?" he asked, and no, she didn't, especially because he was the most exciting thing to happen to her love life in forever. And there was no way she was admitting that now.

He pushed away from the table and faced her, putting his arms down on either side of her to lock her in place. He watched her carefully for a second, as if trying to read her mind and then he leaned in to kiss her.

It wasn't going to stop there. She didn't want it to, not with the memories of last night lingering. She wrapped her arms around his shoulders, her legs around his waist, and pulled him in closer, loving the way his arms felt around her. Her belly tightened, her sex already wet, and God, she wanted him. Now.

"Hunt," she murmured against his lips. "Hunt, please…"

"I don't think I could get tired of hearing you say that," he said. "Hold on tight."

She did, her lips pressing along his shoulders and neck as he carried her back inside the house. He tasted like salt spray and warm sun and she put a hand on the back of his neck to keep him close as he placed her on the edge of the kitchen island, but barely.

"Let's see if you can keep your balance," he murmured as he deftly pulled down her boy shorts, forcing her to hang on to him for dear life. Her bikini top came off next, thrown to the floor, and she was bare in his arms, her nipples erect and longing for his touch.

She loosened her grip on him a little as she gained her equilibrium, only to lose it again when his mouth circled a turgid bud, sucking one then the other until she nearly forgot she was supposed to be holding on.

"Beautiful," he said, moved his head up while his hand stroked her sex, making her moan and thrust back against his fingers.

She held on to him with one hand while reaching in between his legs with the other, which made him groan.

She worked him with the same rhythm his deft fingers used to play into her, a leisurely slide, until she wasn't sure if she could stand it.

Thankfully, he didn't want her to.

"Don't hold back," he said, his fingers deep inside of her, his thumb pressing her clit until she felt herself begin to shatter. She let go of his shaft in order to hold him with both arms around his lower back.

And finally, finally, he entered her while she was still coming—it was, at first, one long, slow stroke that made her gasp and groan with much-needed release. Then he thrust against her hard and fast until one orgasm turned into another as he clutched her hips, pulled her back and forth to him.

His look of utter and complete concentration, his green eyes holding fast to hers made it even better than last night. There was a familiarity she didn't think would be there this soon, a heightened awareness of the way her body responded to his.

She saw in his eyes that she was forcing him to lose all his hard-won control because of the strength of her orgasms, and when he came, he buried his face against her neck and murmured her name.

17

CARLY WAS STILL WRAPPED securely in Hunt's arms, content to stay there all day and night if he'd let her.

"What the heck is that?" he asked. He'd been looking over her shoulder, and she turned to see he had a perfect view into the hallway where she'd hung the key-lime colored dress over a closet door so it wouldn't wrinkle.

She pulled back and he helped her off the counter. "My maid of honor dress," she said as she picked up her bikini and slid back into the bottom.

"Oh," was all he said.

"What do you think?" she asked as he tied her bikini top back into place and reached for his own bathing suit.

"It's just…not you," he said. He walked over to the dress, reached forward to touch the material gingerly, as if the fabric would detonate if held at the wrong angle.

Nothing could help this dress. It had lace and rhinestones and flared from the waist with so much tulle that Carly wasn't sure she'd fit through any doorway without some serious help. "Are you sure you don't want to reconsider being my date for the wedding?" she asked.

"Any chance she'll elope?"

"Not a one. She's in it for the reception. Trust me."

"As long as I don't have to wear anything like that, I'm

in." He smiled, but she noticed he backed away from the dress. "And I'm ready for my lesson."

"I didn't teach you enough this morning?" she teased, and his eyes darkened with that same desire she loved seeing when he was inside her. Unfortunately, a SEAL on a mission was not to be deterred.

"Unless you'd like to head to the wedding in that thing alone," he motioned toward the dress as he walked toward the sliding glass doors.

She followed quickly. The thought of going through the wedding alone was too scary to even consider.

Not nearly as scary as the thought of going near that water, though.

Outside he asked, "Do you want me to bring these down to the dunes?" He'd headed directly to the longboards.

"Not yet. First, we have to talk."

"Talk?" His tone was doubtful. "Carly, no man wants to hear a woman say those words, and we're going surfing. You've kept me waiting for days, and surfing equals action, not talk."

"I thought I was the one doing the teaching?"

He muttered something about stubborn women and sighed like the walking wounded. "Fine. We'll talk."

"Good. Tell me everything you know about waves."

"You're kidding me."

"No, I'm not." Mental pat on the back for the stall.

He frowned and went to the surfboards. "You're stalling."

Admit nothing. "I don't know what you're talking about. You said you wanted to learn about surfing and I'm trying to teach you. I ran an entire school, and I can tell you that the first thing my students did was learn about the sport."

Again, not entirely true, but if she could put Hunt off, make him think this learning process would be boring, he'd give up. "I still can't believe that you grew up around here and you never surfed."

"It wasn't my thing," he said, shrugging a little.

"So you chose a job that put you in the water."

"I didn't say I didn't like the water. Just that I was too busy to put in the kind of time surfing would've needed. And if I can't do something all the way, I'm not even attempting it."

"What were you busy doing?"

He paused. "I worked nights. So the few hours I had between dawn and daylight were either spent sleeping or finishing homework, or finding Ty and dragging him home to sleep or do his homework."

"You don't strike me as the type to do homework."

"There's an awful lot you don't know about me, Carly. And I already know about your whole fear of the water thing, so you don't have to put up a brave front."

"I don't know what you're talking about," she said quietly, as her throat tightened.

You will not cry in fromt of him.

"Admitting the problem is half the battle."

"I don't want to talk about this, Hunt. I mean it."

"Look," he said. "I can help you. Get you back in the water in ten easy steps."

"I'm not a project. And I can fix myself."

"By staying out of the water?"

She stared him down, or attempted to, but he wasn't backing down first. Neither was she. "I can't be fixed with your euphemisms and your SEAL training. I'm not some grunt you can build up with a few words and some overbearing attitude. I'm not that simple."

"No, you're not," he agreed.

"You have no idea what I've been through." She stood, the anger rising hot and hard, the way it always did when she had this conversation with herself. She wasn't sure if she was angrier with herself or with Hunt, but judging by the way she was feeling, he was going to get the brunt of it.

"I know fear. I live with it every time I'm on a mission. It's part of my career, the way it was built into a part of yours."

Her breathing was audibly harsh, grew worse at the way he talked about her career in the past tense. "This whole thing was a bad idea."

"Why? Because you have to face reality rather than run from it?" he asked.

"I'm doing this myself. I got myself into this, I'm the only one who can get myself out of it." She admitted, "I have a lot of fantasies involving you, but being saved by you isn't one of them. Not like this."

Hunt gave her a long, hard look. Then he shook his head and propped the board back against the house, and walked down the path that led along the side of the house to her driveway.

"Where are you going?" she shouted.

"I've got places to be. People who need me," he called over his shoulder.

Carly's stomach clenched as she followed his retreating form, then she curled her body into a deck chair and let the tears of frustration come.

"YOU'RE WORKING TOO HARD for someone who's supposed to be on partial leave." His CO, Captain Jason Andrews, aka Hollywood to his teammates when he wasn't within earshot, drawled over Hunt.

Hunt was doing one-armed push-ups in the gym, working off the mounting tension and confusion that even mind-blowing sex couldn't stave off.

Being saved by you isn't one of them....

Maybe he was the one who needed saving. Since what he hadn't told anyone in his civilian life, including Ty, was the real reason his team had the R&R to begin with.

The real reason his CO had insisted he and Cash, and the other members of the team, take time to get their heads together was that two of their teammates had been so badly injured during their last mission they'd never serve again. Hunt had faced it, dealt with it, had seen the base shrink as they'd all been required to do. He didn't want to dwell on it.

Yeah, he knew about fear.

"I'm fine," he told Jason, gritted his teeth and did another two push-ups in rapid succession to prove it to himself or his CO. He wasn't sure. "Just. Freakin. Fine." He collapsed to the mat, rolled onto his back and stared up at the ceiling.

Clearly his CO wasn't buying it and neither was he. He'd been thinking all day that he should back out of Carly's family's party, before it occurred to him that he'd never crapped out on a commitment in his life. He'd made the decision to show. If she didn't want him there, she could tell him to get lost.

Jason crouched down next to him. "You did your personal best today on the swim."

"I know. And I beat everyone's personal best, too."

"Modesty's not one of your finer qualities."

Hunt grinned. "Felt good out there. Good to be back. We're ready, you know."

"You were never *not* ready. You just have to know that things aren't going to be the same. And that that's all right. Nothing should ever stay the same, or life gets easy."

"Noted."

"So get the hell out of here and enjoy a few hours of peace."

Ah, Jason's way of telling him that today had been the first in a series of readiness drills. Hopefully, he'd make it through most of the party before he got called in for a new mission. He wasn't sure Carly'd understand, it was a chance he'd have to take. A lot of people didn't, and those who did were keepers, as his married teammates attested to time and time again.

"I'll be in Vero," he said.

"With the woman who used to surf professionally?"

"Cash needs to go through basic training again," Hunt muttered.

"He's untrainable, but it's amazing the intel he'll give away when he's trying to get out of paperwork," Jason stated. "Are you very involved with her?"

"Depends on what you mean by involved."

Jason crossed his arms and stared him down, and Hunt let go of the evade-and-escape act quickly. This man had forgotten more about the technique than Hunt could ever hope to learn. "Look, it's a short-term thing. It's not going to distract me."

"Sometimes we all need a distraction or two when it comes at the right time. Where, exactly, will you be tonight?"

"A restaurant off the pier. I don't remember the name."

His CO's eyebrows rose. "Fancy party. Wear your tux."

Hunt had been to plenty of banquets before, and weddings and parties, so he owned his own tux, two of them actually, because not only did Jason insist that every grown-up man needed one, so did his SEALs.

"I'll make sure you've got a ride." Jason's final words were spoken as he made his way out the door.

Yeah, he had a ride all right. One he'd signed on for and now couldn't get off. Between Carly and the job and Ty distancing…

Ah shit. He turned back over and started in with the push-ups again.

SAMANTHA ALMOST GROANED out loud when David raised his hand in the back of the classroom.

"I've got a question, Ms. G," he called, as though she couldn't see his waving arm.

She motioned for him to speak, almost blushing with mild embarrassment because she knew what was about to happen.

"Do you know how pretty you are?" he asked.

She sighed and shook her head. Working with seventeen-year-olds had many, many facets, and crushes weren't uncommon. But leave it to her star pupil to ask this one.

The girls in the class groaned, and most of them turned to David and shook their heads.

"David, let's end this now," she stated matter-of-factly.

"I'm being serious. I'm not hittin' on you or anything, but I'm stating a fact. You gotta know, right?"

They started their careers in seduction so young these days. She began to tell him to cool it when she heard the unmistakable rumble outside her window.

She hoped her students wouldn't notice the noise, since they never noticed things she wanted them to notice, but a six-foot man dressed in black riding a vintage motorcycle was not something this group was going to ignore.

The boys got up to check out the motorcycle, and the girls, to check out Ty. Who she was going to kill. Right after she got fired.

"He says he's here for you, Ms. G," David called out. "And he agrees with me that you're hot."

Well, in her estimation it was more than a little late for those kinds of lines. Days late. A full week of agonizing over what she'd done wrong was enough, she was so done with this dating thing. Not that she and Ty had even had a single date, which might account for the fact that he'd never called or got in touch with her since they'd spent that night together.

At least Carly hadn't said I told you so. And since her friend was still in contact with Hunt, Sam hadn't wanted to lay too much on her. Since, although Carly would deny it, she was falling for Hunt, and why should Carly be affected because Hunt's brother was a total jerk?

Sam sent her students back to their seats with promises of less homework and maybe even donuts in the morning if they could keep a secret. That meant by lunchtime the entire student body would know about Ms. G's secret admirer. Let's hope the teacher population would be slower on the uptake.

She stood by the window, angling her body so she blocked him from crawling through. Her voice was low when she spoke. "Seriously, what do you think you're doing, Ty? This is my job. You can't show up here like this."

"You're pissed I ran out," he said. He looked tired, but no less handsome, his hair worn loose around his shoulders and his dark eyes meeting hers.

"Yes, I am, but it still doesn't change the fact that you shouldn't be here."

"I always do things I shouldn't, Samantha. I thought we covered that the other night."

"We covered a lot of things, but I expected you to at least be around in the morning to say goodbye. I didn't think you'd be the kind to run out."

Ty shifted on the seat of his bike. "I assumed you'd have some second thoughts. And that's okay. You gave me some nice memories."

"What are you trying to pull?"

"I'm not pulling anything. If I'd known you'd be so upset I'd have stuck around, but I thought it'd be easier this way."

"And so you showed up at my school this morning because…"

He paused, checked over her shoulder and then looked her right in the eye. "I missed you. Figured that's not a good sign since it happened after I'd only been gone a few hours. Or maybe it's not a bad sign, depending on what side of the window you're on."

"If you felt that after just a few hours, why wait a week to get in touch with me?" she asked. He bowed his head to the ground for a minute, and when he returned his gaze to hers he still didn't give her an answer.

"David, sit down," she commanded without even looking back. Ty gave a small smile, so David had indeed been out of his seat and approaching the window.

Sam realized she was in big trouble here—on her side of the window. But she'd known that the second she'd met Ty. "I'll see you after class," she told him. "At my place. It's got to be after five though because I have to help with drama practice."

"Am I in trouble, Ms. G?" he asked, with a lot of hope in his voice.

"Let's say that you're in dire need of some after-school tutoring." Then she closed the window and watched through the glass as he rode away.

18

GLASS-OFF, AS IT WAS known in surf-speak, was the period in the early evening when the ocean looked smooth enough to skate on. It was one of the best times to surf, and one of the quietest, too. When the day met the night, dusk settled in and anything was possible.

Now, with the pre-wedding Winters party only two hours away, Carly stood farther beyond the dune than she ever had, pleased with herself that she'd made it this far. Memories of her in Hunt's arms, close to the spot, helped immensely, and she fought to keep her breathing calm. She wouldn't try to get nearer the water now. Instead, toes in the sand, she planned to assess the surf, see if that worked. She'd look at it from a clinical point of view.

Carly checked the fetch of the first wave that rolled in, determining the size of the wave easily with the old equation she'd been taught years ago. Wind speed times time times distance.

Sounds a lot like a ride on a Harley.

Funny how her mind kept strolling right back to Hunt. Equally frustrating was the dopey smile she discovered plastered to her face whenever the tall, blond, handsome SEAL popped up under her memory's radar. She didn't have to try very hard to recall how his hands felt on her, skimming her back, her stomach, moving slowly up her ribcage to her…

She had to concentrate. She watched the fluff spray off the lip of the wave, remembered what it was like to be a floater, riding her board along the foam. She screwed her eyes shut, pictured herself on the face of the wave, carefully judging how far to push before being sucked under. The pitching lip of the wave a surfer avoided like the plague.

She scanned the horizon and pushed down the dread that always accompanied thinking about that day, the moment her career ended and almost took her life.

Her leg ached in tandem with the memory, and then a sharp, biting pain in her heart took the edge off.

Maybe Hunt *could* help her.

"No," she said out loud. She couldn't throw off one dependency for another. Healing herself was the only answer, as much as she wished it could be another, possibly more convenient way.

Tonight, nothing would be convenient, because there was a pre-wedding party to be at and a lot of explaining to do when she didn't show up with the SEAL.

He'd been so angry that morning, stormed off, and she'd realized she still didn't have a way to get in touch with Hunt. She'd have to spend the drive to the exclusive restaurant thinking up a good excuse for why her "boyfriend" wasn't by her side. Truthfully, she hoped he was, so she could tell him about her progress today.

For the first time since she could remember, she was reluctant to turn her view away from the water. A good sign.

She walked slowly toward her house, grabbed her shoes from the bench on the portico where she'd left them next to her small bag and headed for her car.

Hunt's bike was in the driveway, looking very much at

home. He was sitting casually on her front steps, and she hoped the hitch in her breath wasn't audible.

She'd mentioned that tonight's event was formal, and he looked amazing in his tux—relaxed, as if he wore one as often as he did fatigues. His hair still fell on his forehead, making him look the part of the reckless bad-boy that he was. And she wanted nothing more than to hug him for coming through for her.

"I wasn't sure you'd be here," she said instead, scraping the ball of her bare foot on the ground.

"We made a deal. I'm hoping you stick to your end of it," he said and stopped, letting her know he was dropping the subject, at least for the moment.

She pushed thoughts of their argument to the back of her mind and focused on how good he looked. The tuxedo was cut and fitted to the man. Incredible, impeccable… She could also imagine how breathtaking he must look in his formal uniform.

"Whose ride are we taking, anyway?" he asked.

She looked between Hunt and the bike and as much as that would drive her sister just the right amount of crazy, the last thing she needed was to flash the Florida coast-line.

"We'd better take my car." She motioned to her dress, a silky white strapless number she hoped would pass muster with her sister, but Hunt seemed more than aware of what she wore. Even moreso of what was underneath, if the look in his eye was any indication. She wondered how it was possible to be so angry with him one minute and so completely taken with him the next. Then she wondered if he was thinking the same thing about her.

Carly had to face the fact that she didn't know him very well at all in some respects. In others, she knew him very well. And she liked what she knew. Very, very much liked. Liked so much that she wished they had more time before leaving for the restaurant. And, as though he read her thoughts, he took advantage of the fact that her hair was swept up in a loose knot and kissed her neck, then tenderly, her cheek.

"We've got a long drive ahead of us," she said, smiling. "Are you ready for all this?"

"Like I keep telling you, Carly, I'm always ready for anything."

HE WAS LYING, OF COURSE, but Carly didn't know that. He ran a hand gently over her hair. "You look great." More than great. Truly unforgettable in that dress, her shoulders bare and tanned, her skin so smooth. His hand lingered in the softness of her hair and he inhaled the scent of citrus she wore. "Almost too great."

"It's all about control, Hunt."

"I've got plenty of it. I'll keep it in my pants. For the time being."

"Unless you want everyone to know what you're thinking, I suggest you do more than keep it in your pants."

He couldn't resist leaning forward to give her a soft kiss. "The party's not for a while, and I'm just getting into character." Getting into, and planning on staying in it, too, because tonight was all about distractions. He was going to try and have as much fun as he possibly could. And make it as much fun for Carly.

He thought about telling her that he was going to get called out later and decided against it. Knowing that—how much fun could she have? Although he was going to get Carly back on her board. Maybe they'd get close again, too. The way she'd been looking at him when she'd found him on her doorstep implied that she wanted some of that same kind of luck.

"You've got that look in your eye," she said, motioning for him to get into her car.

He thought for sure she'd toss him the keys, but she got into the driver's seat and started the car. "The look that tells me you're thinking very impure thoughts."

"Caught me."

"Me, too," she said, offering him a warm smile.

TY LOOKED READY TO BOLT again, and Sam now knew that wasn't something he did often or willingly.

He must have something on his conscience.

"Hope I didn't get you in too much trouble today," he said finally. They'd been settled at her kitchen table for almost twenty minutes.

"I'm the talk of the school. You made quite an impression on the students."

"I can imagine."

"They want to know everything about you. And so do I," she said encouragingly.

"Samantha, I don't know—"

"You promised me anything if I read you that fantasy," she reminded him.

He groaned. "That's not fair. What you wrote, what you read, that would bring any man down. I'd have promised to sell my Harley the other night for the chance to hear you read it a second time."

"I did read it a second time," she said as he moved toward her, pulling her up from the chair and against him. "And a third time…"

"Why don't we go for setting a record?"

"As much as I know I'd enjoy it, you owe me," she said,

and traced one of the tattoos on his bicep. She looked into those deep, dark brown eyes that got to her so quickly. "We'll start small. Childhood."

"Damn, you're not letting go of this, are you?" He sighed, released her and sat back down. "Hunt worked, I played. That's what I remember most about my childhood."

"What about your parents?"

"Dad left when I was pretty young. So did mom. She couldn't handle the two of us by herself, so she took off when I was about thirteen."

"Did you and Hunt go into foster care or something?"

Ty shook his head. "Hunt never told anyone she abandoned us. He was only fifteen, but he didn't want us shoved in some home or split up, so I tried my best to stay out of trouble and not draw any attention to us."

"That sounds hard. Very hard."

"Hunt found this guy, retired Navy, down the street. He'd stand in as our uncle when an adult needed to show up and talk to the principal. Or the police. He had a lot of connections in the town, and he saved our asses more times than I care to think about. I just tried to have as much fun as I possibly could, and ended up giving my brother more hassle than he deserved."

Hmm, why wasn't she surprised. "Where's your mom now?"

"She died a few years ago. Hunt doesn't know it, but I found her after he enlisted in the Navy and I made my peace with her. She was so young, too young, when she had us. She was only sixteen when Hunt was born." Ty shook his head. "I don't blame her, but I know Hunt does. He would have been pissed at me for putting myself out there like that to her."

Sam stood, went to him. "See, that wasn't so bad, now was it?" she asked softly, kissing his cheek and then his chin and finally his lips.

It was a sweet kiss that pretty much broke his heart.

Sam had no idea just how bad it all was, and it didn't look as if it would improve anytime in the near future.

When Ty had walked the bike away from her apartment complex well before dawn a week earlier, he'd figured that that was it. He'd waited until he was far down the street before he'd hopped on the motorcycle, slammed it into gear and sped off down the slick streets. The tropical rain storm continued to kick up its heels.

He'd veered in between slippery palm leaves and branches and kept an eye out for downed power lines, happy to have something else to think about besides what he'd just done. He'd hit the highway with a fury, opened the choke and took off in a blaze of heat and smoke, figuring he'd left Samantha behind. For good.

Slunk out like a coward. That had never happened before. Ever. No matter how bad the effects of the previous night. And there had been no after effects that morning, only Samantha sleeping soundly on the pillow next to him. Her dark hair splayed, his gut telling him he'd like to do this again and again.

When he'd first opened his eyes and found her nestled against him, he'd been relieved. Then he remembered that he hadn't told her anything. That he'd promised her his secret in the morning. In full lust mode, she had invited him to bed, even reiterated her willingness to go to Vegas with him. But that was the heat of the moment talking. And he hadn't wanted to be there when the harsh-light reality hit in the morning, hadn't wanted to hear her give him some lame excuse.

Welcome to reality, Ty. "There's more, Samantha," he said quietly.

"I know."

"And you're not going to be happy with me that I didn't tell you sooner. Right away."

"Why don't you try me? You already agreed I'm full of surprises."

He held her so he could watch her reaction while he told her. Everything. Told her what he'd come here to tell Hunt but couldn't, hadn't found a way to, yet. Talked until his breathing came harsh and his eyes blurred and Samantha stopped him from talking with a kiss. Then another and another until they ended up in her bedroom and in her bed and in a place where nothing mattered, except the feel of her skin against his, and where he was done fighting for strength.

19

THE GUY WAS TALL ENOUGH, at least six foot one, but no taller, maybe one hundred seventy pounds and decent looking. If you liked the smooth, well-oiled, never-worked-a-hard-day-in-your-life type, that Hunt was one hundred percent sure this Evan guy would be. Judging by what type Carly did respond to, and oh man, had she responded, pretentious, overbearingly polite and, by Hunt's standards, soft, wasn't ever going to do it for her.

"Evan's headed this way," she whispered.

Yeah, and I could take him easy.

"I e-mailed him, but it bounced back. I didn't call him to cancel, either. So he might think I'm his date," she continued, without moving her lips. She gave Evan a polite smile and a small wave because that's where they were—in polite, society-function land. Maybe he should've taken Cash up on his offer to *get that party started* by bringing a couple of other guys from the team along.

"I thought your sister told everyone that I was your boy-friend," he said.

"Some people chose to block that out."

Evan didn't look happy as he sized Hunt up, and he was gaining speed. "I think he's starting to get the message that you're not his date tonight. But, if you want, I could slip out the back door and leave you two alone for a nice reunion." *Over my dead body.*

"Don't you dare," she said, tightening her grip on his arm.

"Then you have to promise me a few more things. And fast, because he's making a beeline for you."

"This isn't fair."

"I never play fair. It's more fun that way." Hunt eyed the side door.

"He's almost here," she whispered. "Name your price."

"I'll let you know after I check out the bathrooms," he said.

Her eyes widened. "Fine. You win," she said. A few of his tried and true evade and escape maneuvers landed them in the middle of a swarm of guests on the other side of the restaurant. Evan was nowhere to be found.

"How'd you do that?" she asked.

"Classified," he said. "One of the perks of spending a lot of time avoiding the enemy."

"Carolyn." Nicole came speeding toward them on impossibly high and stylish heels, dragging her fiancé behind her. "You're late."

"I guess you can't always be successful," Carly said.

"What does your sister do for a living again?" Hunt asked before Nicole got closer.

"She lives to annoy me, pretty much," replied Carly. "And she's also a retired beauty queen. She won Miss Florida last year. And I'm not late," she addressed her sister, who leaned in for a quick kiss.

"You must be Carly's SEAL." Nicole was tall and pretty, with enough of a resemblance to Carly to know they were sisters. But, in terms of everything else, the way the two women held themselves, spoke, dressed, all bets were off. Nicole looked more like an unapproachable ice-princess with her hair pulled back severely and diamond studs as big as marbles in her ears.

"You can call me Hunt. And congratulations on your engagement," he said, taking her hand and giving the back of it a quick kiss.

"I thought you'd be wearing a uniform," Nicole said.

"Only to the wedding. Otherwise, I'm allowed to dress like regular people."

A few more minutes of small talk and Nicole was leading Carly away to talk to other guests. Carly attempted to bring him along, but he excused himself, headed to the bar to get them both something to drink. He was restricted to club soda tonight when he could've used something much stronger.

Nicole was as high-maintenance as Carly was low, and he was tired after spending only a few minutes with her. No wonder her fiancé looked dazed. Poor bastard.

"Heard rumors you're military. I'm retired Army. You a Marine, son?" The man next to Hunt was probably early fifties, in damned good shape, standing against the bar smoking a cigar.

"No, sir. Navy."

"Sailor?"

"SEAL."

"SEAL," the man repeated. "The ones I knew back in Vietnam were crazy."

"Yes, sir. But in a good way," Hunt said, and the man laughed and clinked Hunt's glass with his own.

"I'm David Winters. Carl's brother. The black sheep of the family."

"Don't listen to him." A strikingly pretty woman turned from another conversation, speaking in clipped, British tones. "Just because he didn't go into the family business, he likes to fancy himself a rogue. I'm Susan, David's wife."

"Nice to meet you. I'm Hunt."

"Yes, Nicole's already let the family in on you."

He sighed and wished he could turn water to wine. "That bad, huh?"

"You'll probably be forever known as Carly's SEAL," Susan said, and he really, really hoped Cash never got wind of that one.

"I'm sure Carl's not going to make it easy for you, but you've got one member of the family pulling for you," David told him.

"Make that two," Susan said.

He felt awful lying to them, began to see how bad an idea this was. Sure, he could lie with the best of them when the circumstances necessitated it, but he didn't want to lie to these people. Especially not another military brother. There was a certain code he lived his life by, and a brother in arms was not someone he was comfortable deceiving.

"Carl's been pumping me for information about military deployments and what life with you would mean for Carly," David continued. "It's the most we've talked in years, and the only time he's ever called on my military expertise."

Hunt smiled, wondered why Carly failed to mention that her uncle had been in the service. "What do you do now?"

"I run a private security firm." He pulled a card out of his wallet. "Give me a ring if you're ever bored and looking for a side job. Although I'm hoping to see you more often at these family functions."

Hunt stayed to talk with David and Susan for a while

longer, found his small party joined by a few more people, all curious about who he was and what he did for a living. David smiled the entire time and egged people on while Hunt fielded the military questions, and no, he was not related to the oil Huntington fortune.

He wondered how well it would go over if he told them that his father pretty much drank himself to death after the plant closed. Or that his mom waitressed until she was dead on her feet and held it together for a few years, only to pick up and leave when Hunt and Ty were teenagers.

Even David wouldn't understand that. He was military, but Hunt doubted their pre-boot-camp experiences were similar. Hunt could even tell the party-goers about that terrible day, when he'd just made it through boot camp successfully and found out Ty had cancer.

Hell had taken on a whole new meaning.

Ty's fine now. He would've told you. Yet, Hunt couldn't shake the nagging feeling that there was a lot his brother wasn't telling him. He wasn't sure why folks insisted on trying to keep secrets from him, he supposed it made everyone feel better to think that they were protecting him.

He excused himself and headed into the crowd to find Carly. She'd get his mind off anything the way she looked in that dress.

"Hunt, are you enjoying yourself?" Carly's mother touched his arm before he had a chance to get away and gave a small smile.

"Yes, ma'am. Thank you."

"Please, call me Sheila. I insist." She held her champagne flute by the stem, twirled it between her fingers as she spoke. "I do hope you're letting Carly get some work done on the charity event."

"It's her top priority," he said, having learned a long time ago that playing along was the best way to find out things he wasn't supposed to know anything about. "That's next week, right?"

"Yes. Monday afternoon."

"Right. My scheduling's a little off since I've been on R&R."

"I'm worried that she took on a bit much. I hope she's well enough not to re-injure herself."

So she's running the event and surfing in it. No wonder she's wound tighter than a top.

"She's a professional. I'm sure she knows her own limits," he said. He just wondered if he knew his.

"Will you be there, Hunt?" she asked.

"I wouldn't miss it," he said, knowing that Carly would want to make sure he wasn't anywhere near the event. He guessed that his role as stand-in only pertained to the wedding and didn't extend into Carly's real life and the things that mattered most to her, like surfing.

MISSION AVOID-EVAN WAS successful through most of the evening. Dinner was uneventful, and thankfully, Carly had noticed that Evan's place card had been put at the table next to Hunt's. She'd moved it when no one was looking.

Carly spent time after dinner speaking to relatives and friends of her parents and left Hunt to fend for himself. When she found him dancing with her eighty-year-old Aunt Edna to the song, "Our Love Is Here To Stay," she almost burst out laughing. Evan sauntering to her side ruined the mood.

"Care for a dance, Carolyn?" he asked. "You do owe me for not answering my e-mails."

She really had to learn that escape trick from Hunt

sooner than later. "Sure, Evan. And I'm sorry. I did send you a reply e-mail. I thought my mother told you that I was dating someone."

"Yes. I heard. You'll have to introduce us later," he said, and led her onto the dance floor. "Why is it you never mentioned him before this past week."

"I like keeping my personal life private," she said. For a minute, she wondered if maybe Sam would go for Evan. He was much, much better for her than Ty was. Safe and steady—the type Sam always went for. And truly, there was nothing wrong with Evan, save for the fact that he didn't do it for her. "And I can't believe that you don't have women chasing you down."

He laughed, and yes, he was handsome. Not in the rugged, rough-and-tumble way that Hunt was, but he was refined and elegant. "I can't complain, Carolyn. But I haven't met anyone who measures up to you."

"You barely know me."

"We used to be best friends."

"We were younger then," she reminded him. "My interests are a lot different now."

"Your interests almost got you killed," he said, not unkindly. "I was worried. I called, you never called back."

"I know. I'm sorry. It wasn't an easy time for me."

"I know that you never did like having any kind of fuss made over you. I know you better than you think," he said, and yes, maybe he had taken more time than she'd thought in getting to know her when they'd dated.

"There's more to me than just that," she said.

"If you'd give me the chance, I'd like to know all about you."

To another woman, maybe it would've come off as sexy. Commanding. But after being with a guy who knew the real meaning of the word *command* in so many different ways, Evan's words did nothing for her.

She couldn't help it when her gaze fell on Hunt, who seemed deeply engrossed in conversation with Edna and in no apparent hurry to rescue her.

In fact, he seemed not to notice she was on the dance floor, and when the song ended, he somehow ended up dancing with her sister. After enduring a second song and excruciatingly polite conversation with Evan, Hunt materialized by her side. Carly introduced them, watched as Hunt and Evan shook hands, stared one another in the eyes, neither one blinking until Evan bowed out politely.

"I thought my aunt might've tired you," Carly said, once she was back in Hunt's arms and dancing to a slow song.

"No way. She's got a lot of good stories. Did you ever hear the one about Uncle Horace and the big fish?"

"Shut up."

"Well, since you're not interested in swapping tales, how about you tell me the details of the charity event you're planning next week."

She paused.

"Sounds like it's a pretty big deal."

"I'm just organizing it. It's for a great cause—raising money for research into spinal cord injuries," she said, and he nodded.

"Hear you're supposed to surf."

"I don't want to talk about this. You know that."

"I know that you're not helping yourself. If you can't do it, don't you think you need to set up a replacement?"

She pulled away from him, but he took her back into his arms. "Be careful. You don't want anyone to think there's trouble in paradise."

"What are you doing?"

"Thought you were having fun driving your family crazy?" He kissed her, wasn't surprised when she pulled him in closer as the heat rose between them. But he stopped before either of them got carried away, and for a few minutes they danced in silence.

"Aunt Edna likes me better than Evan," he said finally.

"Aunt Edna thinks Frank Sinatra was her lover."

"She did mention him an awful lot. And she thinks you go to topless beaches and I didn't disagree with her."

Carly started to laugh and saw he wasn't kidding. "You didn't."

"Wasn't that part of our cover story?" His hand slid behind her neck, and with strong, competent fingers he massaged away some of the tension she held there.

"Mmm, that feels nice. Don't stop."

He didn't, leaned in close to her ear to murmur, "You sounded more sincere when you said those words this morning. Although you were louder then—when your legs were wrapped around my waist."

She heard the giggle coming from her mouth, couldn't remember the last time that had happened. "Have I thanked you for coming yet?"

"Which time?"

"I'm being serious."

"I made a promise," he answered, flicking his eyes upward to meet hers.

"So did I," she said, the familiar tension creeping into her shoulder blades.

"And I'm planning on holding you to it. But I think it'll be easier once we figure out how to get you back into the water."

"I don't know how easy it's going to be," said Carly.

Hunt continued his massage of her neck, brought his cheek in to nuzzle against hers. It reminded her of their first night together, when he'd urged her to just let it go. That's how she felt all the time…around him. And before she could stop herself, she was admitting, "It's just that I haven't talked about this with anyone."

"I'm here. And I'm willing to listen."

Carly stared up at him for a few seconds, into those dark green eyes with the gold flecks, and realized how used to him she'd become. Used to seeing him on her beach and in her bed, used to fitting in his arms the way she was at this moment. And when he wasn't there in the flesh, he was in her dreams. "You've already done an awful lot for me, and I haven't exactly lived up to my end of the bargain."

"You did tell me your fantasy," he reminded her. "Loud and often over the last week."

Her cheeks warmed, nipples hardened against his chest and he noticed her response. He seemed to notice everything about her.

"Well, that's been my pleasure."

"Mine, too."

"So is that why you're doing this?"

"Doing what?"

"Worrying about my surfing."

"If you're living with that much fear and you can't push through it, you're not really living. Not on your terms, anyway, and I don't want to see that happen to you," he said.

"It doesn't matter. My career's over."

"It does matter. It matters to me. You matter to me," said Hunt.

Carly really, really wanted to ask him to repeat that last part.

"So tell me."

Maybe it was because she'd had some wine or because he held her so close, but she told him the story, right there in the middle of the dance floor.

That day had been perfect. Carly was confident, perhaps overly so, since she'd been surfing Oahu for three years running, practicing as often as possible on the Pipeline.

Getting older had no real benefits in surfing. You gained a healthy respect for the ocean, but you also had a nice dose of fear instilled in you. But on that day, there was no fear to be found.

Carly had paddled out, away from the crowds, three deep, that formed along the shoreline. The water had been surprisingly cold, but she'd ignored the warning signs.

I'm going to rock this one, she remembered thinking. Others before her lost a few golden opportunities, she noticed, but missed the wave runner that had been dispatched to gather up one of the women she'd surfed with in a prior tournament. Paid no attention to the ambulance sirens because nothing would touch her.

That's the way it had to be.

Carly's first ride had been amazing. She felt as if a glow surrounded her on the slow-motion flow in. She was pumped, her coach gave her the thumbs-up from across the beach and she waxed her stick and dried off, waited for her next heat.

Time to show the young ones that experience does mean something out here.

But on the second ride, things changed. It started out seamlessly when she mounted the board, prepared to ride her wave to victory. She was at the critical section, the wind causing a slight cross-chop, but nothing she couldn't handle. She knew nothing but the thrill and she never saw the haymaker coming.

That rogue wave came out of nowhere—cleaned her and the other surfer in her heat right up. And the tides collided, slammed her down, and she tumbled, her leg flailing helplessly, because the damage to her knee and thigh happened almost immediately. The riptide swirled, pulling her farther under. She hit the coral reef headfirst, blacked out, and was later told how her broken back must've occurred as the tide kept her defenseless body down, under the water, and pounded her mercilessly against the reef.

The next hours were a dizzying blur. Carly'd later learn she had a concussion from where she'd taken a hit by her own board. And she'd needed stitches along her elbow where she'd sliced it on some coral when she'd been thrown to the bottom.

Carly hated the fact that she'd been dragged out helpless before the crowds and the cameras. Thankfully, the published pictures had been tasteful, her image blurred by the paramedics surrounding her. A scary sight indeed, when she had such few memories of those moments.

What she did remember was the pain. Strapped to the board, she remembered trying to free herself to stand and not being able to feel much below her waist. Remembered being so alone.

One of the best parts about being wild and free was not being tied down to anyone and anything. But since then, Carly had started to realize that being tied down wasn't such a bad thing, even as her body flushed hot at the thought of last night's escapades. Strings didn't always mean restrictions. She was learning that on many levels.

"I almost drowned," she said, because he wasn't saying

anything, just watching her carefully. Mainly, she didn't want to be pitied. "I've been swimming since I could walk, because I ended up throwing myself into the pool so often that my parents were forced to give me swim lessons, or keep chasing me, fully clothed, into the pool. So that was the day I almost drowned."

"You never did have control over the ocean. Might've felt like it, but I bet you always knew it was tricky out there."

"I don't like feeling out of control. Not strong."

"But you are strong. Maybe one of the strongest people that I know," he said.

She shook her head no, but he stopped her by cupping her jaw in his palm. She was forced to look into his eyes when he spoke again. "You're strong, Carly Winters. Don't you dare let the fact that you've got a little fear inside of you make you think you're not. There are many definitions of strong."

"It's more than a little fear," she whispered.

"And you're so much more than the sum of your fears. You're a survivor, and before you were a survivor, you went out and made your dreams come true. I don't know a lot of people who can say that."

"That still doesn't get me back to where I was."

"But you're not going back there," he said kindly, but with conviction. "Not in the same way. And that's okay."

"I know it's not going to be the same. But I just want back in."

"And I think I have something that can help."

"A miracle?" she muttered.

"You can have this," he said, handing her what looked like an ordinary woven bracelet, slightly worn and weathered with age.

"What's this?"

"Some juju," he said.

"I don't need voodoo. Come on."

"It's not voodoo, and you're getting mad again."

"Yes."

"So, can we have make-up sex now?" he half-joked, tucking the magic juju bracelet into his pocket.

"Do you take juju with you when you go out on a trip for work?"

"They're called missions, not trips. And I take anything and everything that could possibly help, including common sense. Sometimes tricking yourself isn't a bad thing."

"I don't want to depend on anyone. Or anything. Same as you. And I don't see you telling me about one of your personal failures," she said.

Carly saw some kind of emotion flash in his green eyes, something she couldn't quite place before it was gone. "I didn't think so," she said when he stayed silent. She'd hit him right between the eyes on that one. Even so, she was the one whose upper-arm muscles had tensed as if preparing for a tough swim. "Have you ever been hurt, Hunt? Really hurt?"

"Amazingly, no. But I have been shot."

"Most people would consider that really hurt. I consider that really hurt."

"I recovered. No damage. I can still do my job, so I don't consider it the same thing."

She gave him a quick smile. "I see what you mean."

"Would you go back to it? If you could?"

Carly didn't answer. Couldn't really. More than a job, surfing had been a love, a Zen-like experience. Okay, she couldn't have her old career, but she needed to be out on the water, yearned to feel the waves rushing around her. She needed to regain her balance.

It's all about balance, Carly. Balance and control, her old coach's mantra echoed in her ears.

But she didn't always mind not being in control. And spending time with Hunt had brought that home again in a way that blew her mind.

20

"AND THE HEADPIECES FOR the bridesmaids are absolutely fabulous," Nicole was telling someone as Carly and Hunt made their way to the deck.

"Why am I suddenly having visions of you in a tiara?" Hunt asked.

"You're not far off, from the rumors I've heard," Carly replied. "I'm completely horrified by it, but the pageant thing runs heavily through my sister's world, and crowns are an important aspect of it."

"Are there any beauty pageants in your past you want to share?"

She laughed. "Absolutely not. However, it wasn't for my mother's lack of trying. Somehow, all the dresses she tried to put me in kept mysteriously disappearing or got ripped up."

"Why, Ms. Winters, are you telling me that you weren't always the proper lady I see before me?" he teased, because it was good to see her smiling. After she'd told him about her accident, a weight seemed to have lifted from her. He believed that was a big help on the road to her healing.

"Hard to imagine, I know," she said. "But I was much more interested in playing with the boys, and not in the way your dirty mind is imagining, than walking a runway.

Nicole, however, loved it. She was born to wave to the fans, and after that, my mom pretty much left me alone. In a good way."

"Yeah, younger siblings can do that."

"Did Ty get all the attention in your family?"

"I guess you could say that," he agreed, and turned in the direction of the sudden screams. He was the first one to make it through the crowd to the railing overlooking the beach. The first to catch sight of the swimmers waving their arms madly.

To a casual observer, the girls were having a grand old time. Hunt knew better.

No lifeguards were patrolling this stretch of beach, and the two girls on their boogie boards obviously didn't understand the danger of attempting to swim out of the riptide. Instead of taking a sideways route, they continued to swim against it, trying desperately to reach the shore and panicking as they got tired.

Carly was by Hunt's side in a second and he knew, just knew, at any other time she would've been with him in a race to the water. Dress or no dress.

"They're in big trouble," she said, and saw his arm grip the railing. "You're going in?"

"Yes. But I don't need help out there. Just call 911," he said as he jumped over the railing, caught the stairs two at a time even as he peeled off his tux right down to his boxer briefs.

Good thing you decided to wear underwear today.

Would've been a hell of a show for the Winters, though.

He zipped into the water, took neat, easy strokes when he got past the surf and stayed at least ten feet to the side of the rip. The water was cold, but he was back in the familiar. He approached the girls also from the side, instructed them to get on their damned boards and stay on them. He planned on pulling them out of the riptide and to shore. Of course, they ignored everything he said and tried to grab him when he was close enough. Natural instincts. He had to yell at them to stop, and finally they did what he'd asked.

He swam them sideways until he felt the pull of the rip ebb, and then he tugged them quickly to safety. The girls were fine, only shaken. No more than fifteen, they looked at him with that combination of awe and innocence he'd seen so many times before. And that's when he became acutely aware that the entire party had watched him from the restaurant's deck. In his damned boxer briefs. His strip show had obviously caught the attention of the party-goers and they'd gravitated toward the action. In fact, David was clapping and raising his glass in a toast.

He'd get the old bastard back somehow. Payback among brothers was a bitch.

"Great job out there," one of the EMTs said as he handed Hunt a towel. "We've had about ten calls like this today. Maybe you should ride with us."

"I'm busy, but thanks for the offer," he said.

The other medic checked on the girls, and Hunt wrapped the towel around his waist and took a deep breath.

Carly had kicked off her shoes, but stopped short of the sand. He walked over to her instead of forcing her hand, because hell, he'd caused enough trouble today. She'd told him the story, and he didn't want to push her too far, too fast. Revealing what she had was more than he'd expected, and the fact that she'd trusted him with that secret meant something. They were getting closer. And he wasn't sure if this stand-in thing was morphing into something neither of them had expected, but suddenly, that didn't seem like such a problem.

"They're calling you a hero, you know," she said.

"Nothing a lifeguard couldn't have handled." *Or you, in better times,* he thought, and knew that's why she suddenly looked so sad. He hated seeing that in her eyes, and he took her against him in a tender hug.

She was holding his tux, which started vibrating between them. He swore softly under his breath, pulled the palm pilot from his pocket and gave it a quick look. *Ah, right. The day's not over yet.* "I've got to go," he told her.

"I thought you were on vacation?"

"It's called leave. And I told you, it was partial leave. It means I'm still on call."

"I understand," she immediately said, and although he appreciated her saying that, he knew he hadn't confided enough for her to understand. Not really.

Not like you shared anything about yourself.

She hadn't pushed that issue, and he'd focused on her and her needs, the same way she'd focused on her own needs.

Not fair—you didn't give her a chance to help you with anything.

He hated it when Ty was right, hated it more that what he felt for Carly in this short time was more than he'd ever felt for anyone. Period. Maybe the experience with his men last month had left him craving more, or maybe, maybe Carly was the right woman?

"I'm glad you were here. Really," she said. "And you've blended in great today," she continued.

"What? You didn't think I could handle Evan and a couple of hundred rich people?" He smirked, ran his hand through his wet hair and surveyed the crowd on the upper deck that had formed within seconds of the rescue. "They have sex in the bathroom just like the rest of us."

"No. Who?"

"Yes. And I'm not sharing that information, so keep your voice down. Your parents already think I'm a bad influence on you."

"You are. More than you know."

"Then I'm doing my job right."

"Speaking of jobs," she said, "I've been meaning to ask you another favor."

"Does it involve another fantasy? Because I'm sure that I could sneak you into a private place."

She laughed. "It's about the charity event."

"You want me to come?"

"Could you?" she asked. "I mean, I'm not sure I'm going to be able to surf, but it would be easier if you were there."

He smiled because at least something good was going to come out of this mess of a relationship, or whatever it was. "I guess you could twist my arm," he said.

And then, when she spoke again, everything came sharply into focus. "It's my mother, she thinks you're coming, and I guess it would look weird if my boyfriend didn't show for the event. And I don't want to give her or my father any more reason to compare you to Evan."

Right. For show, Hunt. Don't get too attached.

No, he'd learned that lesson well. In so many ways, he and Ty were alike, except that Ty was more honest about it. But both of them hit the open road with a ferocity that couldn't be underestimated, and both refused to look back except to reach an occasional hand out to the other.

You never had a reason to stick around. Still don't.

"Yeah. Wouldn't want that," he said, trying to keep the bitterness out of his voice.

"Will you be gone long? I mean, do you think you'll be back in two days?" she asked.

He wanted to tell her that in all probability it was merely a training exercise to see how fast the team could get to base and be ready for deployment in a situation where they were scattered, but he couldn't. For all he knew, it was a call about a mission and he wasn't allowed to share that intel either way. All he could do was make contact for a ride and give his usual, vague answer. "I'll be in touch when I can." He punched in a few numbers on the beeper, waited a second and got the response he was looking for.

Carly offered to drive him back to her place for his bike.

"It's okay. I'll catch a ride."

"You don't need to take a cab. Trust me, I can easily walk away from this party."

It was on the tip of his tongue to ask her what else she could walk away from, but he didn't. "I'm not taking a cab," he said, then motioned to the Coast Guard cutter coming full speed ahead to the dock not far from the deck.

She raised her eyebrows. "Good to have friends with fast boards."

"Comes in handy." The cutter maneuvered along the side of the dock. One of the coasties waved to Hunt, and pointed at his towel, calling the other guys on deck to check it out.

Yeah, they'd be talking about this one forever. But at least they'd arrived in the nick of time, since he spotted the news truck parking near the beach.

He took advantage of the moment, figuring it was already too dramatic, movie-of-the-week worthy to not grab Carly for a long, smoldering kiss. When he broke away, she looked slightly stunned, put her hand to her lips.

Uh-huh, he'd given the teenagers something to be in awe of. Then he turned tail and hot-footed it to the waiting boat, tux in tow because at least there, he knew exactly what to expect, and what was expected of him. Cash had been right—the surfer girl was turning out to be more complicated than he'd ever fantasized.

WATCHING HUNT CUT EASILY through the waves had done almost as much for her as having him inside her last night. The same overwhelming sensation flitted across her skin as she recalled those hands cupping her breasts, hers pausing over the hard muscles in his shoulders and upper back, feeling the sheer weight of Hunt massing her.

He'd helped her out by telling her to stay behind, when he knew she could've handled that riptide.

Even though she hadn't known him very long, he somehow managed to get to know all about her without much effort. She blamed it on the stress of the upcoming wedding and the charity event, telling herself she'd never let her guard down so easily otherwise, but a nagging feeling told her it had nothing to do with any of those things and everything to do with Hunt.

"That was some show," Carl Winters said.

"Told you those Navy SEALs were crazy," her Uncle David chimed in. "But I'm glad he's on our side."

"Me, too," Carly murmured, more than aware of the way people were looking at her, talking about her and watching the boat Hunt boarded scoot away over the roughening waters.

She wasn't blind, had watched the women eyeing Hunt from the start of the party. She understood the attraction, moreso now after seeing him in action, but that initial jolt when they'd first met remained in the forefront of her mind.

"Does that happen a lot?" Evan asked.

It was on the tip of her tongue to say, *how should I know?* But she caught herself. "Yes. It's a significant part of his job." And for the first time, she understood how hard that part of his job must be. If she was feeling slightly abandoned and he wasn't even her real boyfriend, she just couldn't imagine.

"Well, suppose he's not around for the wedding?"

"I guess that's something I won't know until the last minute," she admitted.

"I'm not bringing a date. I was hoping to bring you, and I'll take any opportunity I can to show you I'm serious about a future together."

"Evan, we haven't seen each other since last year, and we've exchanged a few e-mails."

"We're perfect together. Our families know it. Why don't you see it?"

She could practically see his cluelessness when it came to her and it held no appeal for her. Her mind wandered back to her SEAL.

"The reporters are here." Carl Winters broke through his daughter's reverie. "They want to know about Hunt."

"She can't tell them anything," her Uncle David interrupted. "Not even his name. These guys live to be secret. You can't announce who he is to the press."

"I didn't realize," she said. Her uncle looked at her curiously.

"I'll handle the reporters," he said.

"Do you think we could bring the focus back this way?" Nicole asked from behind them. "Carolyn, he's not going to do anything like this at my wedding, is he?"

"Save drowning teenagers? I promise I'll tell him to leave everyone in danger so you can have your moment in the sun."

"I'd appreciate it." Nicole pointed urgently to Carly's bare feet then her discarded shoes before heading back to the party. Carly stayed on the beach, watching the last of the early evening swimmers and surfers come out of the water, and wondered when she'd hear from Hunt again.

"HE'S NOT GOING TO TAKE it well." Ty was sprawled across her bed, while Samantha traced the intricate tribal-patterned tattoo that circled Ty's bicep. Next was the Chinese symbol on his shoulder.

"Faith," she said, repeating what he'd told her last night.

"I'm trying, but I know him." He kissed her cheek. "Are you okay?"

Sam nodded. When Ty had first told her the cancer was back, she'd been shocked and sad and angry all at once, and it evaporated as soon as she looked at him. She'd fallen in love with Ty that first night and there was no turning back now. Although he'd put up a good front, he was ten times more frightened that he'd ever admit to. "Maybe if you just talked to him. About everything."

"There's no talking to him. He always wants to solve things. He doesn't want to bow to the fact that he doesn't necessarily know what's best." Ty set his jaw, and she could see the stubborn side of his personality.

"He's family. He wants to take care of you, Ty," she reminded him. "I'd be the same way about Carly—she's the closest thing to family I have."

Ty sighed and stared at the ceiling. "Maybe. Maybe you're right."

"I'm right about everything. You just haven't figured that out yet." At least she could make him smile. She loved it when he smiled like that—at her, for her, it didn't matter.

She wanted to keep him smiling at her forever, never mind that she wasn't exactly sure how long that would be.

"Those are awesome," he said, rising from the bed and stepping into the hallway, where black-and-white stills lined the walls.

"Thanks. I need to get back to my photography," she said. He'd stood and walked over to take a closer look at them. She studied his muscular back, and couldn't fathom how someone so strong could be so sick.

"You took these?"

Sam nodded. "A few years ago. I was really into photography. Thought about making it my career."

"So what happened?"

"It wasn't exactly the most practical career decision," she said.

"You should do it. Just pick up a camera and do it," he said suddenly.

"And if I pick up a camera, what are you going to do?"

"I'm going to Vegas," he said. "And I'm trying to understand why you're the only person who hasn't tried to push me into treatment."

She just smiled. "Why Vegas?"

"I like gambling and I've always been a betting man," he said. "Can't think of a better place to hang out."

"Uh-huh. Nothing to do with a doctor out there who specializes in aggressive new protocol for HD?"

"Son of a—" He caught himself, clenched his jaw. "Nothing's proven. It might not work."

"But it might."

"How can you be so optimistic?"

"I'm a gambling kind of girl." She paused. "You do remember that you invited me along."

"Darlin', I remember everything about our first night

together," he said, then climbed back into the bed with her and pulled her close. "But I haven't decided to get the treatment. Right now, I'm leaning toward no."

"Well, what if I go with you? No matter what you decide."

TY CLOSED HIS EYES FOR a second and thought about what that would be like.

Today he'd told Samantha things he'd never told anyone. Stupid things, funny things, the things you'd share with someone you've fast fallen in love with. Things that should've sent her screaming into the night because taking off on his own, at seventeen, had led him down more than a few paths he probably shouldn't have been on. Skirting the line had become his specialty. Instead, she'd shifted closer to him, as if she was never going to let him go.

When Ty had visited his mom a few years earlier, she told him that she'd embraced the concept that everything happened for a reason, no matter how good or bad. So if he had to hit this kind of bottom to meet Samantha, then that was the way it had to be. "Do you believe in love at first sight? Soul mates?"

"Honestly, I never believed in the concept of soul mates before I met you," she replied.

"'Cause I've been looking for mine my whole life." He turned away from the ceiling to focus on her eyes—dark and comforting—taking him all in. "I can't make any promises, you know, about what I'll do."

"I know. But what can you make promises about?"

"I told you the way I feel about you. For me, that's the most serious promise any man can make. And it's not because I'm sick and need someone around, because trust me, this is the worst time to get involved."

"Or maybe it's the best time. Either way, I think we're about to find out."

He sighed, ran his hands through his hair. "If you're with me out of some misguided sense of loyalty…"

"That's not it. I'd never do that to you."

"Then why?" He grabbed her, brought her to him urgently. "You've got to tell me why. Until I know…"

Sam quieted him with one kiss, then another, until there was no space left between them. Her body moved against his, fit there perfectly as it had that first night, which held such promise. Ty knew she wasn't going to give up on that promise.

"I think you made me believe in soul mates. Weren't you the one who told me I had a wild streak hidden inside me, waiting to come out?"

He grinned, stroked her bare hip gently. "I guess I did. So what's your plan?"

"The question is, what's *our* plan?"

21

TY WASN'T HARD TO FIND. As much as he loved the freedom of the open road, whenever he was in Vero, Hunt knew he could usually be found in one of three places—the diner, Magee's or a garage fixing up his bike.

Today, Hunt found him in a local garage, working on his Harley. Music was blaring in the background, so Ty didn't hear him come in. Hunt had to turn down the music before Ty looked up from the wheel base he was greasing.

"Hey. Haven't seen you much since the other night." Ty smiled but he didn't stop working, which Hunt didn't see as a great sign.

"Same," Ty said.

Hunt grabbed a beer from the cooler on the ground and waited. Soon enough his team would be gone again, leaving precious little time to deal with things on this end. "Carly had some family party. I had to go to it with her."

"Were you a hit with the parents?"

"Hardly. I'm not exactly what the moneyed set had in mind for their daughter."

"Surfer girl's rich, huh?"

"Her family's rich. I guess she's doing okay."

"What's a rich girl want with a grunt like you?" Ty asked.

Hunt took a long pull of his beer instead of laughing like he was supposed to.

"Sorry, bro. Didn't realize it'd be a touchy subject."

"It's not."

"Whatever you say."

"Dammit, Ty." He threw the bottle into the trash bin across the room. "Don't start with me."

"Sorry, Jon. Calm down. You used to be able to take a joke."

"I used to be able to do a lot of things," he muttered. "Are you really taking her with you?"

Ty finally turned from the wheel he was fixing. He wasn't wearing a shirt and he'd wrapped a navy-blue bandana around his head. There was a beer bottle by his side and a variety of tools. "Can't go anywhere without her."

"Be serious."

Ty stood. "Samantha's different. Truly different."

"Different's not your thing."

"It's not like I'm kidnapping her or anything."

"You aren't promising her anything, either."

"I don't have anything to promise anymore," Ty said, his voice tight, and Hunt knew exactly what he meant.

For a second, Hunt's life as a SEAL flashed in front of his eyes. It was more than ironic, since he wasn't the one who was dying. "Dammit, Ty—"

"What are you promising surfer girl? You can't promise anyone tomorrow, either."

"I'm promising her a date to a wedding. And I can't help it if my job's dangerous, but that's not the same, and you know it."

"I'm not talking about your job, which, by the way, is much more dangerous than me taking off on my hog any day of the week. I'm talking about your life."

"Let's talk about your life, instead," Hunt said quietly, needing to hear his brother say it.

After a long pause, Ty confirmed Hunt's worst fear.

"The cancer's back." His brother chewed his bottom lip for a second before he spoke again. "The doctors say there's a chance I could beat it. If I want to try."

"What do you mean, if? You've got to fight this thing, you're going to fight this thing if I have to tie you up and drag you to the hospital myself."

But Ty was shaking his head. "Maybe this is the way it's meant to be, Jon."

"Screw you. And screw your philosophy." He started to walk away, but Ty got in a parting shot, and one that stopped Hunt cold.

"You can't control everything, bro. No matter how hard you try."

"Just watch me," Hunt said.

Ty responded by throwing an old muffler directly at his head, but Hunt didn't care.

"You pick some woman and decide she needs an adventure rather than taking time to care for yourself? What the hell's that all about?" Hunt demanded, happy that for once, Ty wasn't all cool and composed. Since that's how it usually worked. Hunt got angry and Ty would just smile.

"I prefer to think that Samantha picked me, and that I'm the one headed for the adventure." Ty's jaw was tight when he spoke, but he met Hunt's eyes.

"Cut the crap. You need to go to the hospital, not strut around like some bad-ass without a care in the world."

"Is that what you think I'm doing?" Ty shook his head, walked away and took a few deep breaths.

"You're making the wrong choices."

"And you have control issues. You pick needy women to fix so they can stand on their own, and then you're off again in search of the next one. I may wander the open road, but you're the one with wanderlust in your soul. You get frustrated when you can't solve everyone else's problems. Well, you know what? You can't solve someone else's problems. And you shouldn't have to. People who solve their own are that much stronger for it, but I guess you're not looking for somebody strong, an equal. Why should you, when it's easier to concentrate on someone else's life than on your own, easier to stay in control than to hand over the reins?"

"I did that. Handed everything over, and look what happened."

"Sometimes you do have to trust, Jon."

"I just want you around."

"And I want you happy. Settled."

"Ty, I'd…"

"I know you'd do the transplant for me again. But it almost killed you last time. I couldn't watch you go through that."

"You don't get to make that decision."

"Actually, I do." Ty shrugged. "And I haven't made it yet. Not completely."

Hunt sighed with relief. The people around him were trying to kill him. That was the only reason he could think of for all of this.

"What are you going to do, Jon? Let Carly lead you around like some pretend member of society? Are you having fun now?"

"You don't know anything about it."

"I know you're falling for her. Hard. And what's she doing for you?"

Hunt didn't know how to answer that. Hell, she was doing something for him, but he wasn't sure exactly what.

Hunt said nothing else to Ty, simply turned and left and had no clue where he was supposed to go.

CARLY HADN'T BEEN ABLE TO sleep, so she spent most of the night writing her article.

She tried to tell herself that the insomnia wasn't because she hadn't heard from Hunt. And before she knew it, two days had passed, without a word from him. She checked in with Samantha, and Ty hadn't heard from him, either.

This is what it's like sometimes, Ty had told Sam, who'd relayed the message to her the morning after Nicole's party, because Carly and Ty were still on shaky ground. *Jon just drops out of sight and then shows up again. I'm sure he's okay. I know it's a pain that he can't tell you much, but you'll get used to it.*

The thing was, she very much wanted to get used to it. She liked thinking that Hunt might be around a lot longer than she'd anticipated because suddenly, she couldn't picture herself without him. Was it possible for her to fall for someone so fast?

When Carly heard the bike roar up in the driveway sometime after five in the morning, she had to force herself not to run out and meet him. But when ten minutes passed and he hadn't rung the doorbell, she went downstairs. Once she opened the door, she found him standing, balanced against the bike, looking off into space.

"You're early, even for the dawn patrol," she said.

"I'm not here for a lesson," Hunt replied.

He appeared tired, rumpled, as if he hadn't slept in the two days since she'd seen him. "Are you okay?"

"Fine. I'm fine," he said. "Spent the night riding."

He was scaring her. She knew that the words *Hunt* and

control were synonymous. Right now, he didn't look like he had a grip on anything.

"Why don't you come inside? I can make you some breakfast," she offered, holding out her hand to him.

He glanced at it tentatively for a second, then stuffed his hands into his pockets.

"I'm not hungry."

"Please, tell me what's wrong."

"Nothing. Everything. I shouldn't have come here," said Hunt.

"But you did come here." She held out her hand, and this time he did take it. Took it and wound his fingers through hers, and even though his hand was larger in size and strength, she felt as if she was the one holding him up.

"Sorry I had to leave the party like that."

"I understand."

"No, you don't. Not really." He stared at the horizon for a second, then back at her. "Is Samantha still planning on going with my brother?"

"Last I heard. She's been pretty wrapped up with him, even put in her resignation. She's describing meeting Ty as a life-altering experience. I guess I can't argue with her anymore, since bike week seems to have changed my life, too." She laughed, but Hunt cut her off.

"He's sick, Carly."

"What do you mean by sick? He seems perfectly healthy to me, and Sam hasn't mentioned anything."

"She knows."

"Hunt, what is it…"

"He's got Hodgkin's disease."

"Cancer," she whispered, as though not saying the word loudly would make it not so real.

"Yes. He's been in remission for a long time, but when we were younger he was very sick. For the past four years, he's refused to have the annual tests he's supposed to. It was almost like he knew." He paused, wiped his eyes angrily with his palm before continuing. "It was like he knew it was coming back and he didn't give a damn."

"Maybe he was scared."

"I told him I'd go with him. Hold his damn hand if that's what he wanted. Anything to check that this nightmare wasn't happening all over again."

Hunt stood, brushed away her hand and her worry. He kicked the step angrily, then looked up at the sky. "He's a stubborn son of a bitch."

"Maybe he can beat it. There are so many advancements today."

"He's not sure he wants to try!" he yelled, startling himself, and when he spoke again, his voice was low. "He's thinking about not getting treatment. Says he wants to live out the rest of his life his way, not stuck in a hospital full of tubes and medicine, not sure if he's going to die anyway."

There was nothing for Carly to say. Her heart ached for all of them—Hunt, Ty and Samantha.

Carly was helpless to make any of this better, and so was Hunt. That's what was killing him the most.

"Come inside," she urged, but he shook his head and started walking along the side of the house, toward the beach. She followed, not able to stand the thought of him being alone right now.

He kept walking, shoulders tense, eyes on the horizon, and so it didn't register that she'd gone far beyond the dunes until it was too late. Her toes hit the sand, and for a few seconds it didn't make sense because she was so intent on her goal of not letting him go. Then it hit her and she stopped. Her breathing was audibly harsh, her heart beat staccato and the thin, familiar sheen of sweat covered her forehead.

And he was still walking, hadn't turned around. She couldn't keep her eyes on him anymore, since her view contained his body framed by the crashing waves—it almost brought her to her knees.

Almost.

A man is dying, and he's brave enough to keep on living. And she couldn't even make it a few feet on sand. Dammit, she was alive.

Her hands fisted so tightly her nails bit into the soft flesh of her palms, and still she clenched them harder, forced herself to draw in a few gulps of precious air.

One step, then another and another and she was farther along, maybe ten feet from Hunt and from the ocean, and she couldn't go any closer, sank down into the sand.

He was turning around, coming back, walking toward her. She forced herself to stand up and she took another step. Then he was picking her up and carrying her. She buried her face in his neck and chest and breathed in his scent as though it were the pure oxygen she needed to survive. And right now, it was. Tears ran down her cheeks and she was sure she was sobbing, and all of this was a drama Hunt didn't need.

But she needed him so much, and he didn't seem to mind, because this was something he *could* do, something he *could* help with. His arms held her tightly, and he didn't say a word, but his heart beat almost as fast as hers against her cheek.

He'd turned around for her. And she'd met him in the middle. Now he was taking her the last few steps, pushing her to go all the way.

The sound of the water grew louder. She bit down hard

on the urge to buck out of his arms and run, then heard splashing and realized he hadn't stopped when he'd reached the tide. Instead, he was taking them both straight into the ocean fully clothed.

"Hunt, I don't think…" She barely heard her own voice above the roar of the ocean, or maybe it was the roar between her ears.

"Then don't," was all he said before he kissed her, hard enough to make her head spin and her heart pound, made her forget about the way the water rushed around her, or the fact that Hunt stood waist deep, past the breakers.

They kissed until she couldn't stand it anymore, until she wanted him to take her right there in the middle of everything, until she had to get herself naked and have him do the same.

Until she forgot she was still in the water. Without thinking, Carly pushed away from Hunt to reach for his jeans, and he let her go. For a minute, surrounded by the cold, blue waves, she forgot what to do. Froze up. Then natural instinct kicked in, took away that heart-in-her-throat panicked feeling and she treaded water. And she smiled and laughed and Hunt was laughing with her.

She was halfway between a combination of exhilaration and crying, part relief and part exhaustion. She dunked her head under the water, stayed completely submerged for a moment, back where she belonged. Carly came up sputtering for air and Hunt was waiting for her, watching to make sure she was okay.

"Are you all right?" he asked.

"For the first time in a long time." Like forever. But she didn't say that. Instead, she took a few strong strokes toward him and took him in her arms. "You'll be all right, too."

It was his turn to bury his face in her shoulder and they

stayed, holding each other up in the swelling waves until she was shivering and the tide had begun to build.

All too soon it was time to return to shore.

Now, she swam in on her own, and together they walked back up the shoreline toward her house.

Carly wasn't surprised when Hunt tossed her over his shoulder and brought her up the stairs and into her bedroom. When he dropped her on the bed, the intent in his eyes was unmistakable, and took her breath away, because he wasn't bothering with formalities or romance. He was counting on a high you could only achieve when thinking ceased and action took over.

She was more than willing to go along with his ride, didn't have time to catch her breath before he was on her pulling off her wet clothes and throwing them aside.

Hunt spread her thighs and kissed his way down her stomach, incited by her moans as he reached his destination. His mouth trailed the inside of one thigh, then the other. He teased her until she begged him and finally his mouth found her core, already hot and wet.

He buried his tongue inside her. She gripped his hair, the sheets, the headboard as his mouth took her so singularly, so purposely that it nearly rocked her off the mattress.

Her first climax came fast and hard, and even as her body struggled to recover, he was taking her there again, holding her thighs open even as she struggled, partly wanting him to stop yet needing him not to.

That only served to intensify his goal. Hunt moved his hands to grip her hips and pull her closer. He didn't stop, laved her already sensitive clit until the next orgasm built, and when his palms reached up to knead her breasts, she let go, lost sight and sense of everything around her as she yelled his name over and over.

A few minutes later, she was vaguely aware of him shifting positions, and he spoke to her urgently.

"Ride me. Hard," he murmured, still managing to make it sound like a command, and oh, that always did it for her, especially when he looked at her. His green eyes were vulnerable with need, and she knew he only wanted her. He'd come to her today, and that was what mattered.

Hunt maneuvered her on top of him and she straddled him, her legs still quivering. He was big, and when she took him inside, she welcomed that first pinch followed soon by the pleasure of him filling her.

"Like that?"

"Yes, Hunt…please," she moaned, because every sensation was heightened, every touch made her shudder.

"Yeah, that's it, baby…love it that you're always so wet for me."

"Only you," Carly whispered, and he rocked his hips up to drive himself farther into her. She was on top, but she knew he was in control.

He pushed her slightly, she put her arms behind her, rested her palms on his hips. And then she moved slowly into his thrusts, head thrown back. She heard his groans, heard him calling her name. Everything got louder and louder. She was sure the entire beach could hear them.

And then Carly leaned forward, put her hands on his biceps and she took over. She covered his prone body and let loose, not giving him any room as she moved against him.

Hunt held off as long as he could. Thought about rolling Carly over and taking her another way, any way, that gave him the top back, but she wasn't going to have it, held him inside her and had her way.

She didn't take her eyes off him the entire time she took him. And she did take him, body and soul, and he knew, absolutely, that he could love her. Probably already did, too.

Hunt closed his eyes, ignored the sudden tandem ringers for his cell phone and beeper, and for that moment, let his imminent orgasm take him away from any more thinking.

22

HUNT HUNG OVER THE SIDE OF the Zodiac 77 SEAL boat. Half of him skimmed the water while he concentrated on staying as low as possible. His wetsuit was uncomfortable. He'd prefer to strip down and take in this day and this storm unencumbered, but practicing drills in the right equipment ensured success when the chips were down.

The boat gathered enough speed in the rocking waves, so Cash gave the signal and Hunt let go. He dropped off the raft's the side in one sleek movement. Into the ocean he went with nothing more than his wetsuited self and a knife strapped to his upper arm.

Hunt remained under for a minute, kicking to the surface in front of the drop point and away from the boat's wake. Then treaded water in the chop.

Fifteen minutes and they'd be back to pick him up. Fifteen minutes to keep afloat, be calm and recon the beach in his sights.

Fifteen minutes he didn't have to think about Carly.

He couldn't disengage. What started as a full-on fling morphed into more, despite every alarm and wall that came screaming down around him.

He didn't remember the drive to Carly's house after Ty told him the news, just knew he had to talk to someone. And the first person who popped into his mind was Carly.

Not good.

At least his cell phone beeper, and this exercise, got him out of her house, and fast, this morning. No time for explanations.

Block it out, he demanded of himself, and he won in the mind-over-matter debate. At least for the moment.

The boat cruised in stealth mode toward him. With the motor humming strong but quiet, he hooked his arm through the pulley and hauled himself up when it passed him. He reported his intel to his Senior Chief over the radio, then clicked off and let the rain slam him.

"Looks like we might go as early as next week," Cash called over the motor, now running full speed ahead. "And you look like hell."

"Feel like it, too," Hunt admitted.

"As long as you match. Want to go out and forget all about it?"

"Can't. Got someplace I need to be," he said. "Have a drink for me, though."

"The mood you're in, I'll need the bottle."

Hunt didn't disagree. "What's on for tomorrow?"

"S.E.R.E. stuff," Cash said.

Survival, Evade, Resistance and Escape. More practice to keep their minds sharp, given what had happened last month. A put-up-or-shut-up kind of situation, so their CO could see who might need a more permanent kind of R&R. Because a hesitant SEAL was no SEAL at all.

"The whole day?"

"I heard talk of forty-eight straight," Cash replied, and his hearing was notoriously correct.

"I can deal with that. Don't feel much like thinking," Hunt said, saw the look of concern on Cash's face. "Ty's sick again."

"Shit."

"Yeah, my thoughts exactly. Now I've got to convince him to get treatment."

"Does Jason know?"

"Not yet. Figured I'd deal with this once leave is officially over. Meanwhile I have a few other commitments I need to figure out."

"Speaking of commitments, how are things with surfer girl?" Cash asked, and Hunt just snorted. "That badly?"

"You know what? At the moment I can't tell if I want things to be good or bad," he said.

"I hate to say I told you so."

"Then don't," Hunt muttered. He'd taken all sorts of risks in his life, but love wasn't one of them. Until now. Now, he couldn't shake the sensation that maybe he was falling. And hard. And maybe she wasn't. "I like her, Cash. I mean, I didn't expect it to happen this way, but I really think…"

Cash held up his hand and shook his head. "Come on, man. You're enjoying it because there are no strings, because there's a built-in expiration date on this so-called relationship. You don't feel the collar of commitment choking you like a noose."

"Dammit, it's not like that. Remind me never to ask you anything about relationships again."

"Honest, I hate to see a friend go down like this." Cash said. "How does she feel about you, anyway?"

Hunt shrugged. "No clue."

"Well, she must like something because she keeps coming back for more, right?"

"She needs a date for the wedding."

"She's not going to keep your sorry ass hanging around if she didn't like you, you know. She wouldn't keep inviting you back into her bed, which is the problem.

You're thinking with your head and not your head, if you know what I mean."

"Enough. Over. I'm through talking about it," he said. Maybe Cash was correct, because every time Hunt saw Carly, all he wanted to do was get her clothes off and make each single thing in her life better.

Cash was grinning.

Hunt swore he'd heard humming to the tune of VanHalen's "Get This Party Started," so flipped his middle finger. Cash laughed, and they both stood in the driving rain.

"OF COURSE HE TOLD ME." Sam sat on Carly's couch, legs tucked up under her, looking somehow more relaxed than she'd ever been.

"How can you be so serene? I don't understand." Carly stood up and began to pace. How was the earth still on its axis when things were this crazy around her? It had only been two weeks, and here Samantha was going away with Ty. Granted, Carly knew she'd hop on the back of Hunt's bike and ride off if he asked her, but Sam was different. She felt like checking her best friend for tattoos.

"Carly, everything's fine. I think he'll try for treatment. I talked to the doctor. There's a really, really good chance everything will be all right."

"That's wonderful. It is. But you're giving up your life here for him. Are you sure?"

"I'm not giving up anything. I'm taking an opportunity. One that I probably never would have thought to take if it weren't for your example."

"My example? I'm so confused."

"Come here." Sam motioned for her to sit next to her on the couch, and Carly did. "Look, when we were in college, I already knew you were the bravest person I'd ever met. You left everything behind to pursue your dream and you succeeded."

"Uh-huh. I'm a huge success." Carly felt the tears rise.

"Stop it. You are. You're back in the water and you'll work out what to do next. But I've finally worked out what I want to do next."

"Ride cross-country on the back of the world's largest vibrator?" Carly joked, and they both giggled.

"Yes. With a wonderful man who's encouraging me to follow my dreams."

She looked into her friend's eyes and she remembered. "Photography."

"I've been sneaking in some classes here and there, and my instructor said I have a natural talent."

"So you can travel and take pictures and be free."

"Yes, and I get to do it with the most interesting man I've ever met. I'm really, truly in love, and I never thought it would happen to me. Now that it has, I can't just stop everything because he's sick."

"How'd you get so smart?"

"I have a great friend."

Carly bit her bottom lip and sighed. She'd never had to worry about pleasing anyone but herself for as long as she could remember. She'd picked up and left school, her parents, everything, for her career. It had been the right move at the time, to be sure, but it had cost her in terms of developing relationships. In terms of figuring out who to get close to and how to stay close.

There was an old competitive professional surfing adage that said, *friends on land, enemies in the water.* Problem was, she couldn't live her life with that kind of attitude, and she'd drifted far enough away from the surfing crowd because of it.

Even her so-called relationship couldn't be deemed one.

With Samantha, her need for Ty seemed to come out of the blue, but maybe it hadn't, really. Maybe Carly had been so involved in her own problems that she hadn't bothered with Sam's feelings. Or Hunt's. Or even her own.

"I've been a terrible friend," Carly said.

"No, you've been focused on your life and what you wanted. Your career. My life was a lot simpler. Still is, I guess."

"How can you call what you're doing simple?"

"It's simple when it's right," Sam said. "Now you and I need to find a way to help Hunt and Ty help themselves."

"First, I've got to find a way to help me and Hunt," she muttered.

"So you've figured out that the stand-in boyfriend has the potential to be the real thing."

"It wasn't what I was looking for. It's all so complicated, and things were starting to get so much better."

"Maybe you're complicating things," Sam said.

"This was supposed to be about fantasy. Make-believe. Pretend boyfriends and getting me out of a jam."

"Well, you certainly got more than your share of fantasy."

"It's that I think…no, I know, I've never felt like this. About anyone. I try to picture what will happen after Nicole's wedding is over, and I can't."

"Because you don't want to. And you haven't wanted to from the second you laid eyes on the man."

Carly sighed. "You knew that as soon as you saw us together, didn't you?"

"Yes. But I didn't want to scare you. Now it's up to you

to decide how badly you want the real thing," Sam said. "You've gotten everything else you wanted, right? Back in the water."

Carly couldn't argue with her friend. She was, for all intents and purposes, where she wanted to be—back in the water, but she certainly wasn't in control anymore. Certainly not over her feelings.

23

THE DAY OF THE CHARITY event for spinal cord research remained overcast. The waves weren't anything close to competition form and Carly didn't care. She'd ditched the formal clothes she'd worn for the meet-and-greet portion of the afternoon and pealed on her wetsuit. Then she paddled out and caught a ride, which wouldn't have earned her much from any judge, but when she heard the yells of the girls who'd been watching from the shoreline, saw them pumping their arms in the air as Carly got closer, she couldn't stop smiling.

Surfing was like riding a bike, and even though her thigh ached during it, Carly didn't care, had welcomed the pain the same way she had over the past days along with the salt water spray in her face and the inevitable wipeouts.

The first one was the hardest, and she'd forced herself to quell the fear and remain under the rolling waves for a little longer than necessary to regain her sense of underwater balance. She concentrated on letting her body detect the flow of the current, on holding her breath and following the leash around her ankle up to her board. And when she surfaced, she found she'd instinctively headed out deeper, away from the break of wave and into the calm, flat water.

She'd welcomed it because she'd missed it, because she

knew Hunt was there, watching her, despite all the other things he had going on in his life. And though she'd done it on her terms, he'd helped to take her over the edge.

Carly climbed back on her board and watched the other surfers she'd joined for the sunset ride finale paddle out for the next break. They'd welcomed her in with the peace sign, and if they'd recognized her, they didn't let on. She welcomed the anonymity. It had never been about the acclaim for her.

It had always been about the ride. Thanks to the event, she'd gotten her stride back. In her professional life, anyway. If she could only reach Hunt as easily, she'd be golden again.

Although, in the eyes of the girls who surrounded her, she already was. She spent an hour getting them on the board and paddling out with them. None of them wore bathing suits and none of them cared that their clothes were soaked or their hair was messed.

And she knew, in those moments, that she could still surf and teach, knew she'd written her last article for the magazine. From now on, she'd make sure the surfing school she'd planned to open got written about instead.

CARLY HADN'T BEEN IN THE water alone, but she'd stood out like a beacon. Set apart from all the other surfers, she shined, and not because she was the hottest one there.

She'd made it look so easy, although Hunt knew by the well-used workout equipment he'd seen in her office and his own tries on a board, with Cash yelling instructions at him moments before he got pummeled, that it was far from it. Even for the months Carly'd stayed out of the water, she'd stayed strong, had rehabbed, had fought to get herself to where she'd been. And she'd gotten there.

All because he'd let his guard down. Now she was back and he was left wide-open, vulnerable. He hated every second of that feeling, of knowing fate was forcing his hand again.

You'd think you'd learn by now about the control thing.

Ah hell, he'd never liked being taught much anyway. Always seemed to prefer the learn-from-your-own-screwups school of life.

"Hey," Carly called from behind him. Hunt had almost cleared the beach and was at his bike when she caught up to him, still wearing her surfing gear and wrapped in a towel.

He'd planned on staying longer, but since she'd seen him before her event, knew he'd kept to his commitment, he didn't think it mattered if he left. "Hey," he said. "You looked great out there."

"Thanks. It felt great," she said.

Keep it moving, Hunt. "Look, I've got to go," he said, motioned toward the Harley and took a few more steps away.

"You can't run away from this and hope it'll all go away."

He laughed, stopped with this hand on the seat because he was so close to escaping. "Pretty funny, coming from you. I'm not running, at least, not from something. I'm needed someplace."

"And what do you need?"

He wanted to tell her that he needed her, wanted her, in spite of everything that was going on, but he couldn't. Watching her conquer her world, seeing her hang out with her old surfing buddies made him feel worse than ever. And though he didn't want to be a major downer on her day, or tell her this in the middle of a parking lot, he had to tell her sometime.

Cash always advised giving women bad news in a public place to avoid scenes, although Hunt wasn't sure when or why he'd decided to take love advice from his teammate.

"What I need never seems to matter," he said. "And I'm tired. Tired of fixing things, making people feel better, figuring a way out of the situation for everyone and their mother. I'm done with it."

"What are you saying?"

"Everyone's on their own from this point out. It's the way it should be, and it's the way it ends up, when all's said and done." Hunt'd been walking as he talked, had picked up speed and now he straddled his bike, as if he was prepared to shoot away from her.

Carly put her hand on his arm, leaned against him so that wasn't possible. "I didn't ask you to come in here and fix me in a two-week whirlwind."

"I know." He spoke quietly, avoided looking at her for the first time since she'd known him. "I brought all that on myself. So now, I go back to my life and you go back to yours. That way, we're all back to where we started— the way it should be. No more pretending. Life's too short for make-believe, anyway."

She wasn't at all where she'd started. And, as much as she loved this new place, she didn't want to relish it alone. "Don't I get a say in this?" she asked.

"You wanted to surf again. That was your dream, and you got that. Or you will, as soon as you can stop talking to me, wax your stick and get out there."

"Were the SEALs your dream?" Carly asked, desperate to keep Hunt here and keep him talking. She couldn't imagine what he was going through since his news left her cold.

Keep him here, and talking. Maybe you can help him.

"Not at first," he replied. "The service was a way to a steady paycheck and decent medical benefits for me and Ty. Just in case."

"And then?" she prompted, seeing Hunt as a young man, dealing with all of this on his own.

"And then I got bored, wanted more action, more of a challenge. Ty grew up and went out on his own and there wasn't anybody left at home for me to worry about on a day-to-day basis. Met a couple of SEALs who talked me into giving BUD/s a try," he explained, then looked up at the sky. When he started talking again, it was more to himself than to her. "Dammit. I knew this whole thing was a bad idea from the start. Told myself not to get involved, that I needed time on my own to get over last month."

"What happened last month?"

"Just something I've got to deal with by myself," he said. And it was back to his usual state of control.

"I'm guessing that there's more to your R & R than meets the eye."

"Guess you could say that."

"What happened?"

"Things I can't talk about, or want to," he said. And he actually moved her hand off his arm and started the engine, letting it rev a little in the open air.

Carly put her hands on the front bars of the bike as though she was hanging on for dear life. "You told me that you'd been shot. Was that recent?"

"No. But if what you're asking me is, have I ever really been in danger, the answer's yes. Every time I go away. And the last mission I went on put me right in the middle and I wasn't able to help my teammates the way I needed to."

"Did men on your team…"

"Die? No, but men got hurt. So badly they'll never be on active duty again."

"It's not your fault."

"That's what they keep telling me and the others who didn't get hurt. And I know that, but sometimes, it's not enough."

"I know," she said softly.

"Yeah, I guess you do," he said. "Dammit, I didn't want to do this here. Didn't want to do this period."

"You came here. To me. That has to mean something."

"It means I honor my commitments, nothing more," he told her, "because that's all I can deal with it meaning right now."

"So that's it? You're ending things like this? What happened to the other commitments you made to me? The rehearsal, and the wedding?"

"I'm sorry," Hunt said. "But I think you're strong enough to deal with your family on your own."

And then he revved his bike and took off out of the parking lot, while she clutched the towel around her and fought the urge to get into her car and follow him.

24

IT WAS TIME FOR CARLY TO get her life under control. The pieces were slowly starting to fall into place, but her familiar impatience began to rear its head in a big way now that she was back in the water.

Nothing at all to do with the fact that Hunt ditched her. After another night came and went without hearing from him, she'd taken advantage of the dawn patrol, let her body meld with the waves and clear her mind.

Then she went inside and went to work.

The first thing she did was quit her magazine job, felt that weight lift off her back immediately. The next phone call was to the owner of the small surfing school nearby. She'd heard rumors that the man who ran it wanted to sell and retire, and she'd always been a believer in fate. It was time for her to branch out again.

The final call was to Pat, her physical therapist. And he was more than thrilled to be losing her as a customer. At least a weekly one. She promised to see him once a month, for a while, to make sure she was still progressing.

The rest of her day didn't go quite so well. It was almost time for the curtain call on Nicole's big day, and Carly had no date for the rehearsal. She did have an easy out—she could tell her family that Hunt was called in, but it would have hurt to have said that. She wanted it to be true so badly.

How had this one thing spiraled so out of control as everything else was coming together?

"Your pantyhose has a huge run down the back of your leg," Nicole stage-whispered, halfway through the evening.

"No way." She turned to check her calf, because this was the third pair she'd ruined. To add insult to injury, she was only wearing them because her sister had told her to. Her hair kept falling out of the neat knot she'd tied up earlier in the evening, she'd spilled wine on the front of her dress and broken a heel from her shoe, and now her sister stared at her as if she were a mutant.

Being asked where Hunt was every five minutes wasn't helping.

Her hero, was how they referred to him, and the majority of dinner was a blur of questions. Although she did do a pretty good job of E & E. Hunt would've been proud.

"So where is that hero of yours?" Aunt Susan asked.

"Classified," Uncle David said, giving her a wink, and she thanked him with a smile for the save. "Don't worry, you'll get used to it soon enough. And to him shipping out."

"It'll never be easy, honey. But every homecoming's like another honeymoon." Susan gave Carly a reassuring pat on the shoulder. "If anyone's strong enough to handle a man like Hunt, it's you. Remember, they need us a lot more than they let on, but they'll never, ever admit it."

"You sure picked a winner," her uncle said to her, his voice low, and she knew exactly what he was thinking. "Or should I call him a ringer?"

Carly gripped the stem of her wineglass and tried to decide if she could still play this off. But when she met his eyes, she didn't see anything but understanding. "How did you know?"

He smiled. "You both had me fooled, up until the press came by, after Hunt's act of heroism."

"Because I didn't know about keeping his name private," she said.

He nodded.

"Anyone who's serious with a Special Ops guy would have to know that. It counts. But you were both very convincing in every other way. I'm sure I'm the only one who knows."

"Uncle David, you can't tell my parents."

He laughed. "I won't. Letting your father think you and Hunt are the real deal is what's making this wedding hoopla bearable."

She was about to respond when Evan's voice carried over the din. "So where is the man who saved the world? Since, if it were me, I'd make sure you were never alone."

Carly fought a groan and ignored the comment, even as her uncle whispered, *give 'em hell.*

"Hi, Evan."

"How about a dance?"

"Sure," she said, let Evan put a hand across her back and lead her to the dance floor.

"So, should I assume that we're on for the wedding?" he asked.

"Actually, no. We're not on."

"But your boyfriend is obviously not around, and your parents and your sister won't be happy if you go to the wedding alone."

"They'll have to deal with it, then. I'm not only Hunt's girlfriend when he's in port," she said. And she meant it.

Now, she needed a plan.

CARLY KNOCKED ON THE door to Samantha's apartment, wasn't surprised when Ty answered, considering his bike was parked in the lot.

"Hey," he said. "Sam's not here. She had some last minute things to go over with the teacher who's replacing her."

"I know," Carly said, accepting that Ty could see right through her anyway. They'd called a tentative truce, but she knew he didn't trust her motives. Not totally.

"Oh." He paused. "Want to come in?"

She nodded and Ty moved aside. She felt a lump in her throat when she saw the packed bags by the door and wiped a tear from her cheek quickly.

"Hey, she's coming back," he said quietly. "I promise."

"I know. You'd think I'd have gotten used to this, but it was always me leaving, not the other way around."

"I understand. But I'm going to pay for the place for the next couple of months so she doesn't have to worry about renting it out or anything."

"Do you think you're coming back here, then?"

Ty shrugged. "I'd like nothing better, Carly. But I can't predict the future. If things go well, yeah, we'll be back. But you didn't come here to talk about me and that's okay."

She sighed. "I'm worried about you and your brother."

"It's strange about Jon, how he always thinks he knows what's best for everyone. Thing is, he doesn't know shit about what's good for him." Ty paused. "But I think you might."

"Do you know how I can get in touch with him? He's always come to me."

"Sounds like him."

"That's not completely his fault, Ty. I haven't exactly been asking him what I could do for him."

Ty stared at her for a minute, then finally gave her a small smile. "Yeah, me neither. He puts up a good front, doesn't he?"

"He sure does."

"He's not answering my calls, and I don't have his work number, since it's a secure line. But hey, how did you two first get in touch?" he asked.

She smiled at the memory.

"Hold that thought," Ty said, "I think I may have a way." He dialed his phone. "Sully, it's me. You see Cash around lately? At the beach—you're sure?" He hung up. "This is going to get good."

THERE WAS A LONE SURFER out in the waves. Carly watched from halfway down the beach, wishing it was Hunt and knowing that no one picked up surfing that fast, no matter how talented they were. There was another storm brewing, so for surfers the waves were killer right now. Still, she couldn't help but worry that whoever was out there shouldn't be surfing alone.

Carly looked up and down the beach for Cash and didn't see him, so she moved in closer to witness the surfer take a ride through a tube she would've killed for. The surfer came out of the curl smiling and waved to her.

In a few minutes, Cash strolled from the water to her, board under his arm. "Hey, surfer girl," he said, brushed wet hair away from his eyes. "You're early."

"You were good out there. What about the bet you made with Hunt, that you could learn to surf faster than he could?"

Cash laughed. "I hope he didn't use that one to get you

into bed because I've been surfing since I was three. Although this isn't my thing." He motioned to the crashing waves. "I do mostly tow-surfing when I can."

That made sense. She could understand Cash's need of being dropped inside a massive twelve-foot wave from a helicopter or dragged by an outer-board. The danger inherent in big-wave surfing would be a match for him.

"I'll kill him," she muttered. "As soon as I find him."

"I'd like to be around to see that."

"Well, that's part of why I asked you to meet me. I've got a proposition for you."

Cash leaned against the board he'd propped in the sand. "Tell me more. Even though I've got a feeling Hunt's going to kill me for whatever I'm about to say yes to."

25

HUNT PUNCHED THE BAG UNTIL it broke. And then he punched it some more, even as sand drained from it and the soldier who ran the gym gave him dirty looks from the safety of the office. And then he jogged to the showers, let the water run over his back in a last-ditch effort to just goddamned relax.

He was going to relax even if it killed him. And, if this kept up, it was going to.

Go with the flow. Take it easy. Stop worrying about everyone else. When he looked down and saw his fists clenched, he knew it wasn't working.

Son of a bitch.

He wondered how many body blows one man could handle before he went down, and realized he was on the verge. All the training in the world wasn't helping right now, and he needed to get his head on straight.

He got out, suited up and headed for his CO's office. Jason sat at the meeting table, a mountain of paperwork in front of him. Funny thing, he didn't look very relaxed either. Maybe it was catching.

"Sir, have you seen Cash?" Hunt asked.

"He got a fax and started mumbling something about Candy and Valentines. Said he'd spend the afternoon surfing up near Daytona," Jason said.

Not if I get to him first. "Thank you, sir," Hunt said, was on his bike thirty seconds later heading down the highway. When he got to Carly's house, he didn't stop to think, just stormed up to her place and rang the bell, once, twice, and then pounded on the door.

Yeah, this take-it easy, go-with-the-flow approach to life was really working out well for him.

Carly answered the door about two minutes later, and he noted first, with relief, that she was dressed and didn't appear out of breath.

"Where is he?" Hunt demanded, holding on to the door jamb for dear life so he didn't storm into her house. And why the hell was she smiling when he was so apparently pissed off?

"What are you doing here?" she asked, and he was done fooling around.

"Tell Cash to get his ass out here now."

"Why don't you come in and tell him yourself?" She moved aside and motioned for Hunt to follow her and he saw red.

He walked in bellowing Cash's name. After the third time, he stopped because he knew that Cash would never break the unspoken code and that he'd never hide from a fight. A nice ruse, and Hunt had fallen for it, hook, line and sinker. Like a jealous fool.

He was still going to kill Cash, though. Take whatever body parts were left over, after Jason got through with him, and finish the guy off because he had to be involved in all of this.

Suddenly, instead of leaving, which is what he should've done, Hunt sat on the back of her couch and shook his head.

Carly was trying to hold back a smile and wasn't successful.

"Nice job," he said. "You got me here. So what's up?"

"You're very good at, what did Cash call it? E & E?"

"Evade and Escape? That's my specialty."

"I thought you didn't run from anything."

"I don't. I'm not. We've been through this, Carly. This was supposed to be a way for you to prove something to your parents and you did that. But I'm tired of being the stand-in." He paused.

"Suppose I told you I wanted you as more than a stand-in?"

"You told me that's all you wanted."

"And you told me you didn't want anything more than a few nights of fantasy."

"I didn't. I don't. Look, you got your life back, Ty's happy and it's time for me to head to work." He stood and got the surprise of his life when Carly pushed him hard, palms flat against his chest.

"I'm not letting you run out on me again, Hunt. So you'd better get used to it."

HUNT LAUGHED FOR A SECOND, supposedly at the absurdity of it. He moved Carly's hands easily from where they remained flush against his chest.

When she'd pushed him, she hadn't even made a dent, but the tone of her voice begged her seriousness. She wasn't letting him out of here without a fight and she was betting he didn't have much fight left in him.

"The first night we met," she began, "you asked me…no, you told me, that I needed to learn to have fun again. You were right, even though I didn't want to admit it. Now I'm telling you, I think it's time for you to have fun."

"I had fun. I have fun. Dammit, it's different for me.

While you were out raising hell, I was raising Ty on my own," he said.

His jaw was tight, his shoulders set in a stance she recognized all too well.

"I didn't have time for fun, Carly, because I had responsibilities."

"And now?"

"Now I just want…" he faltered, trailed off and shook his head. "I don't know what the hell I want. It's never been about me."

"Maybe it's time that it was," she said. "You worry more about Ty's future than your own."

"Without Ty, I'll be alone. I guess I'm trying to live the way I do so I stay used to being alone. I don't like having the rug ripped out from under me."

Nobody did, but Carly saw immediately that for Hunt, that scenario was the worst thing that could happen to someone who was used to being, and expected to be, in total control of a situation.

"You wanted to hear another fantasy," she said finally, ready to give it all she had.

"Carly, I…" He stood, made a move that indicated he'd leave at the next opportunity.

"It involves you not interrupting at all." She walked over to him, pushed him back on the couch with a force that clearly surprised him.

"I'm not in the mood for games."

"What are you in the mood for?" she asked.

Hunt paused, looked her up and down and his body turned complete and utter traitor. The rise in his pants was unmistakable. "How could you want something so much at the same time you didn't? Nothing made sense anymore," he murmured.

"The game is called Yes."

"Never heard of it," he said gruffly. "Is this another Candy Valentine special?"

"As a matter of fact, it is. And I understand you're a fast learner, so you shouldn't have any trouble if you follow my directions."

"And if I don't?"

"Let's say that neither of us will be very happy. And I don't think that's what you want."

"Carly, I…"

"All you have to do is answer yes to every question I ask you."

"Sounds stupid," he mumbled. Although Hunt looked as if he may have changed his mind when Carly lifted her tank top over her head, exposing bare breasts with thin tan lines from her bikini.

"Are you ready to play?" she asked, her voice husky, cheeks slightly flushed. His obvious arousal gave him away; he was more than ready.

"No," he said.

But she'd stopped listening to him, leaned over him so her breasts were close to his face. "No touching. Or kissing," she said when his mouth attempted to make contact with her nipples in a homing-device fashion. "Not until I say so."

"You didn't tell me that part of the game."

"It's not fun if you know everything up front," she whispered, pulled his T-shirt over his head and using her tank top to tie his hands behind his back.

"You didn't say I'd be tied up," he said.

"A big, strong SEAL is scared of my restraints?"

"I didn't say I was scared," he scoffed. "Scared, my ass."

"Now, are you ready to play?"

"Guess so."

"Already not following directions. I see trouble in your future. Are you ready to play along?"

"Yes."

"Good." She urged him to his feet and pulled his pants down slowly, freeing his erection.

"Do you want me to touch you?" Carly asked Hunt.

"Hell, yes," he whispered.

"Still not following directions, so you get nothing," she said, stretching her arms over her head to give him a full view. Goddamned, he was going to rip the T-shirt off his wrists and tie her down and show her what was what if she didn't stop this soon.

"You're playing with fire, baby," he whispered again, and he knew, by the way she looked at him, that she got it. Carly wiggled her hips a little and her lips curved and man, this was hard. Very, very hard. And then she drew close to him again and he inhaled sharply as she ran her hand across his abdomen.

"I know all about playing with fire, Hunt, so don't bother trying to warn me. And I asked if you understood."

"Yes," he said, his voice thick and almost unrecognizable.

"Good. Do you want me to touch you?"

"Yes."

Her hand circled his cock, fingers cool against his hot skin, and he bucked slightly at the touch. She moved her hand up and down his shaft slowly. "Do you like it when I touch you this way?"

"Who wouldn't?" The hand stopped. Oh, crap. "Yes, Yes."

Her finger teased the tip of his shaft, ran along the underside, and he groaned, completely in her power.

"Much better." She smiled, bit her bottom lip and went back to stroking him. When she stopped, he protested and then concentrated on her sexy maneuver to slip her shorts off instead.

She stood in front of him naked and stared at him head to toe. "Do you want me?"

"Yes."

"And you'll do anything I ask tonight to get me?"

"Yes." He was starting to sweat despite the air-conditioning.

Carly used one hand to trace his nipples, then flicked each one lightly with her tongue. She chuckled a little when he jumped and he willed himself to stay still as she continued. But he couldn't stop the growl that came deep from his throat. "Carly, please. Cut this out or else…"

"Or else what? You're going to lose if you don't play the game right. And you want to play, don't you?"

Hunt gritted his teeth so hard his jaw ached, because she'd palmed him again and he'd do anything, say anything, as long as she didn't stop now. "Yes."

"Good. Very good. Sit back down," she ordered, and when he followed her direction she sank to her knees in front of him. He growled again. "Now tell me, do you like to lose control?"

Every inch of Hunt fought a silent battle, waged a war so primitive he could barely draw breath. And Carly watched him carefully, waited for his answer.

"Yes." The word was barely a gasp, but it was out. Her head dipped, her tongue flicked the tip of his cock and Hunt bucked at the touch, though he forced himself to stay seated. She rewarded him by taking him, inch by devastating inch, into her and then swirling her tongue around the tender underside of his erection so it was encased in the unbelievable warmth of her mouth. He closed his eyes and put his head back and let her take him until he couldn't hold back his groans, couldn't stop his hips from moving to the rhythm she'd set. It would be so easy just to surrender to whatever she wanted, but a part of him wouldn't bend to her game completely.

"Oh yeah, don't stop."

She pulled away, wagged a finger at him. "You're not particularly good at obeying rules, are you, sailor boy?"

"Told you, I don't like that nickname."

"Why not?"

"Because I'm a man."

"So I see." Her gaze was appreciative. "But a man's got to learn when to let it all go. When to press on and when to accept going over the falls gracefully." Her finger traced a maddening path along his stomach, up his chest, ending with her breasts at eye level. Carly straddled his lap. At mouth level. At the perfect angle to caress one perfect bud with his tongue...

"Yes," he managed and then repeated it for emphasis. "Yes, yes."

She bent lower and he captured her nipple in his mouth. Her moan was low, guttural, and she grabbed the back of his head to keep him there.

Hunt couldn't believe how far she'd pushed him. How far would he let Carly take him? Would he let her go all the way? Could he?

"Do you like to touch me?"

"Yes."

"Then do it. Touch me. Any way you want," she murmured.

26

HUNT'S RESTRAINTS WERE OFF in seconds, and Carly was under the comforting heat of his body, first pressing her heavily into the couch cushions, then rolling with her onto the floor. She lay pinned beneath him, but able to wrap her arms and legs around him as if she was never letting go. This was good because she wasn't planning on it anytime soon, even after this was over.

Given the way Hunt was touching her, though, it was going to be over sooner than later.

"Do you like that?" he asked after he'd pushed in with one long stroke and took her breath away.

The man had good hands, good everything, and she heard the begging tone in her voice. "Yes."

"You want it fast? Hard?"

"I want anything you've got to give me. I can take it."

He groaned, rocked her back and forth at a pace she had to hold on tight to keep up with, felt his heart beating against her chest as he filled her over and over again, backing out almost completely before plunging back into her.

Carly closed her eyes and came, harder than she'd ever come in her life, yelled his name and various other things that shocked her when she heard them. She felt his release and the tension drain from his shoulders when he half collapsed on top of her. For several minutes, they just lay there on the carpet, catching their breath.

She kept her arms wrapped around him, even as he tried to roll off her.

"I'm crushing you."

"No, you're not. Stay where you are," she whispered.

"A minute," he conceded, rested his head on her shoulder. "Then I've got to go."

"I didn't hear your beeper."

He lifted his head and stared at her. "I don't know how this got so crazy. I don't know what you want from me."

She wanted…everything. "I want a lot of things. But let's start with this. You've handled me broken…can you handle me fixed?"

"Are we still playing the Yes game?"

She smiled. "I'd like a real answer. Not one fueled by thoughts of sex."

"Men are fueled by thoughts of sex most of the time."

"You're avoiding my question," Carly said, because she wasn't letting him get away with this.

"I don't know what I can handle these days, what I want to handle." Hunt tugged away from her and stood.

She followed suit, stood skin-to-skin with him, since she refused to disengage from the physical contact.

"You're going to have to give me some time," he told her.

"I'm afraid if I let you go, I'll never see you again." She brushed her chest against his arm, kissed his shoulder, but he turned, almost roughly, and broke the contact.

"How are you going to handle me away all the time?"

"I'd like the chance to find out," Carly said, even as he pulled on jeans and handed her her clothes. "You don't have to go. I don't want you to go."

"Where can this lead? Your family will get bored with this hero bit soon and remember that I'm not rich. Not even close."

"I'm not like that." She didn't want to waste time getting dressed, just grabbed a blanket from the couch and wrapped it around herself like a sarong. "And it's not about the wedding anymore. It hasn't been for a while."

"You like this because it's an adventure. It's different. But soon my hours and time away aren't going to work for you." He stood, ran his fingers through his hair. She could tell his emotions were raw.

"Why are you telling me how I feel? I'm independent and I don't need constant reassurance."

"I don't know many people willing to wait for their spouse to come home, not knowing where they are, and when, if ever, they're coming home," he said. "And I don't expect that from you."

"You don't expect it? Or you don't want it?" she asked, point-blank. The expression on his face softened slightly, and she held her breath.

The phone started to ring.

"Aren't you going to get that?" Hunt asked.

She shook her head impatiently. "Let it ring." The machine picked up and she heard Evan's voice.

Her first instinct was to run and grab the phone, but she was too late.

"Carolyn, it's Evan. I wanted to tell you that I've been thinking about our dances last night, all night, and that I'm very happy you've decided to go to the wedding with me. Maybe this is finally the start of what was meant to be."

The phone clicked off and Hunt stared at it as if his eyes were a heat-seeking missile. She expected the phone to self-destruct at any moment. "It's not what you think," she blurted.

"It's exactly what I think. It's what I thought the whole time you put your ruse on for your family. It's what I told you the other night, that you and I wouldn't work." He stopped. "But I guess you already determined that on your own."

"I told Evan he could be my date if you got called away, the way you were at the party."

He laughed, a short, harsh sound. "Yeah. That's perfect. Make sure you've got a back-up mate for the times I'm gone."

"That's not fair. Look, this is confusing for me. I needed a date for the wedding, and now I'm falling…"

"Don't," he said, with all the command he could possibly put in his voice. And it stopped her cold. "Don't say it."

"It's true. I've fallen so hard for you."

"It's lust. Nothing more. Things like this don't happen quickly."

"I didn't need more than two minutes on a surfboard to know the sport was right for me. And I don't think I'm wrong that you're starting to feel the same way about us."

"I can't do this now," he said, stood and paced for a few seconds like a caged lion seeking escape.

"Hunt, wait…"

"I don't belong in your world. Never did. But I can't say the ride hasn't been a blast." And then his beeper and phone rang at the same time—like a not-so-subtle reminder that his life was all about leaving on a moment's notice.

"The wedding's tomorrow," she reminded him.

He shook his head. "I can't. Tell your family that I got

called away to duty. So none of them have to know any better, or you can always bring Evan, just the way they wanted you to from the start."

"I don't want Evan. I want you," she stated, with a fierceness that startled even her. She could publicly continue the ruse, but that wouldn't repair the damage to her heart. And really, it hurt much worse than her surfing injuries combined, much, much worse than she'd ever thought possible.

Hunt didn't look happy, either.

Maybe he hadn't fallen in love with Carly the way she had with him, and maybe she'd been wrong about everything. Still… "I'm falling in love with you," she said simply. It was true. She didn't know what else to do, except say it. If that couldn't keep him there, nothing could.

He didn't respond, and was out the door before she had a chance to blink. Carly wrapped her arms around herself, sank to the floor and realized, as the sobs came, that now she knew what drowning felt like. And this time, who was going to save her?

27

THE FIRST THING HUNT DID was hug his brother. When he broke away, he hoped they could both hold it together.

Ah hell, who was he kidding? He was the one falling apart. Ty seemed to be handling all of this in stride.

Your younger brother's one hell of a man.

"You're going to keep in touch this time, right?" Hunt asked. "I've got permission to give you the number for a secure line. That way, no matter where I am, someone can get in touch with me if you need me."

"I've been thinking about that. Thinking it might help if you were there," Ty said. Hunt bit his tongue because it was on the tip of it to say, *I told you I'd be there and you told me no.*

"Ty, when you said you wanted to do this on your own, I took that at face value. Planned on giving you exactly what you wanted, so I didn't take more leave."

"Hey, that's okay. I understand," Ty said.

Hunt stared at him for a second and then shook his head. "You don't have to invite me just so I'll feel needed, you know," he said, and Ty just laughed at being caught. "You take good care of him," Hunt told Sam. She nodded and slung her arms around his brother's waist.

"Will you be taking good care of surfer girl?" Ty asked.

"So, you're leaving tonight?" Hunt talked over the end of Ty's sentence.

"Samantha," Ty began, "I need a few minutes alone with my brother—to beat the crap out of him."

"Not even in your dreams," Hunt replied, as Samantha went back into her apartment.

"What's up?"

"Ty, don't start. Concentrate on yourself, okay? And let me worry about me."

"I've made that mistake before and you couldn't handle it. Don't screw this one up."

"I can't promise her anything. And I have to be at work. It's better this way."

"Keep telling yourself that and one day you might start believing it," Ty told him. "Go on. Get out of here before I say anything else."

"Be good," Hunt called as he started up his bike.

"Brother, I'm never any other way."

On the highway, Hunt's beeper and cell went off simultaneously, just as he was deciding whether to take the exit that would lead him to Carly's or follow the road back to base. He accepted that it was a sign, and pointed himself in the direction of whatever trouble awaited him and his team, and didn't look back.

CARLY WASN'T GOING TO BE able to walk through the doorway. Seriously. She'd tried three times, and each time she felt the pull as the delicate tulle fabric snagged.

Damned crinoline. Like there wasn't enough poof in the dress already.

Finally, with great frustration, she gathered up as much of the poof as she could and shoved herself into the room where Nicole was doing her last-minute primping.

"What happened to your hair, Carly?"

"What? Nothing."

Her mother sighed as if Carly was a small child who couldn't be trusted not to get dirty. There was enough truth to that, so Carly didn't bother to defend herself. She'd gotten in an early morning surf and waited as long as possible for Hunt to show before she made the drive up the coast by herself.

I'd planned to let your SEAL walk down the aisle with you, Nicole had said when she opened the door to the hotel suite and found Carly standing there. And then her sister had guided her wordlessly over to a chair, gathered up ice packs for her puffy eyes and forced her to eat some toast. And then, she'd listened. On the morning of her own wedding, Nicole sat with her for an hour and listened to Carly bawl her eyes out while she choked out the whole story.

And then they'd gotten ready together, and they'd even giggled a little when Carly climbed into her dress. And when Nicole put hers on, Carly's tears had started again.

Her sister had redone her makeup for her without saying a word.

"And I've paired you with Evan," her mother was saying to her as she helped to adjust her sister's mile-long train. "He said you refused to be his date, but you're both here on your own, so what's the harm?"

Nicole had been the one to tell their mother that Hunt had been called away because Carly didn't want to deal with the fallout. Didn't want them to think she was open to Evan's advances, although it was obvious the original plan hadn't worked at all.

"Honestly, I'm not sure why you would want to put up with Hunt's military career," her mother continued. "His job makes him unreliable, and that would drive me crazy. You need some stability in your life."

"Carly's not you," Nicole said, and Carly turned to see a warm smile coming in her direction. "And Hunt's more reliable than most people I've ever met."

Her mother looked surprised, and she didn't say another word. Still, Carly put a hand up to her hair unconsciously and began to fix some loose strands that escaped the knot the hairdresser had arranged.

"Leave it. You look beautiful," Nicole told her.

"Thanks," Carly said.

"And?" Nicole asked and pointed at herself. Carly and her mother looked at one another and laughed.

"So do you, honey."

"A beautiful bride," Carly agreed. "And mother, I'm walking down the aisle alone. Hunt's the only one I'd want to take that walk with. I don't use stand-ins. Not anymore."

"Nicole, please talk to her."

"It's time," her sister said instead, because she'd noticed the tears that had formed in Carly's eyes. "You'll get through this," she whispered.

"I know," Carly replied, but really, she didn't think so.

CARLY STOOD BY HER sister's side through the ceremony. Judging by the look on Nicole's face when she saw her soon-to-be husband, Carly realized that her sister did understand love. She might've chosen a man who would appear on the society pages, but she hadn't compromised. She'd just chosen someone with common interests. And it was apparent that the groom felt exactly the same way.

Carly fought tears through most of the nuptials, mostly happy tears for Nicole and miserable ones for herself, and then took the long walk back down the church aisle alone, and escaped into the safety of the waiting limo.

Wedding ceremony down. Reception to go, and she'd be free…and alone.

The crowds mulled inside the reception hall while Nicole and her new husband held court on the receiving line. Carly broke away from her duties briefly to chat with other family members, wondering when she could safely take off the pantyhose that were strangling her thighs.

Aunt Edna had momentarily cornered her against the punch bowl when Evan came by and took her arm.

"Guess I rescued you," he said.

"I can take care of myself." She didn't like the feel of his arms around her. Evan wasn't a bad guy, but he was so completely wrong for her. Every man was wrong, except for…

Don't say his name.

"You seemed to enjoy being rescued by your sailor," he continued. "What was his name again?"

"I don't want to talk about him," Carly said.

"Even better. After all, everyone always said that you and I were meant to be together."

"So, if we were to be together, I'm assuming that you wouldn't mind if I returned to surfing."

His eyes widened, and yes, it was obvious that he more than minded. "I thought you'd retired. I thought you weren't allowed to surf anymore."

"Not professionally, but I am planning on opening my own surf school. So I'll teach and surf, maybe even enter a few local competitions. That wouldn't be a problem for you, would it?"

He nodded slowly, as if he was trying to decide how to approach the subject. "Would you have time, Carly? You're going to have so many other responsibilities."

She pushed his hands off her waist, but kept her voice low when she spoke to him. "You really think this is it? Me and you?" She motioned between them. "Marriage isn't a corporate merger, Evan. It's about mutual respect, passion and love, and I don't think you feel any of that for me. And I'm certain I don't feel any of that for you."

"Carolyn, please."

"I'd prefer it if you called me Carly. And that you didn't assume anything about me anymore." Evan turned red and walked away, leaving her surrounded by happy couples on the dance floor.

"I guess I'm guilty of some assumptions myself."

The voice was low and deep and for a second she couldn't even turn around, because she wouldn't allow herself to believe it.

"Carly, please face me," he asked her.

And she did, finally, to find Hunt standing before her in full, gleaming dress whites, looking more handsome than she thought possible.

"You came," she said, because she didn't know what else to say.

"Well, I made a promise."

"Oh. So you're here as the stand-in?" she asked, felt her heart grow heavy.

Hunt pulled her against him tightly. "I told you, I'm done being the stand-in. I thought you wanted the real thing."

"I do. But you mentioned the promise…."

"It was a promise to myself. To not let you go without a fight."

Carly tried to say something, but the words caught in her throat. So she reached up and tugged his head down toward hers. She kissed him as if she was never going to let him go, and she wasn't.

"Carolyn, please." She heard Nicole's voice, saw her sister standing next to them. "It is my day, remember. No offense, Hunt." But Nicole was smiling, and she winked at Carly.

"None taken. But I'm hoping you won't mind if I borrow her. We've got someplace we have to be."

Nicole looked between them, then leaned in and gave Carly a quick kiss on the cheek. "Go ahead."

Outside the reception hall Hunt stopped and freed her hair from the clip. "I'm sorry I wasn't here for you."

"Out saving the world?"

"Actually, yes. And doing some thinking, too. Thing is, I might not know where my future will take me, but I know I want it to include you. I want you there by my side."

She stroked his cheek, felt the tears rise again, but this time, they were from that good place, and she let them. "I'd like that, Hunt. I'd love that. And to think, this all started from one innocent fax."

"From what I recall, it was not innocent. I think I fell for you that very first day, surfer girl." He traced her cheek with his finger, and then smiled that killer smile that almost dropped her on their first meeting. "Carly, I do love you."

"Say it again," she said, and he laughed and kissed her instead. A kiss that did tell her, over and over.

When he pulled away, he asked, "I know you're opening your school, but do you think you could push it off for a couple of weeks?"

"I think I could manage that. So, where are we headed?"

He grinned. "Vegas."

"What about saving the world?"

"The world can live without me for two weeks. It's time

for some real R & R. Time to make sure everyone's okay. And after that, I'm not sure," he said.

"After that, how about we figure out the next step together? There's something to be said for living day by day."

"And there's something to be said for looking toward the future."

"Balance," she said. "It's always about the balance."

"You're right, baby, you're absolutely right."

Carly could hear applause coming from the reception, but all her concentration was on the man beside her. A man for whom she had respect and passion, one who wanted every part of her, for better or for worse. As she slid onto the bike, she knew it without a doubt. Theirs was a love here to stay.

* * * * *

Don't miss Cash's story—available from
Harlequin Blaze June 2007!

Set in darkness beyond the ordinary world.
Passionate tales of life and death.
With characters' lives ruled by laws the everyday world
can't begin to imagine.

n●cturne

It's time to discover the Raintree trilogy...

New York Times *bestselling author*
LINDA HOWARD
brings you the dramatic first book
RAINTREE: INFERNO

The Ansara Wizards are rising and the Raintree clan
must rejoin the battle against their foes, testing their
powers, relationships and forcing upon them lives they
never could have imagined before...

Turn the page for a sneak preview
of the captivating first book
in the Raintree trilogy,
RAINTREE: INFERNO** by **LINDA HOWARD
On sale April 25.

Dante Raintree stood with his arms crossed as he watched the woman on the monitor. The image was in black and white to better show details; color distracted the brain. He focused on her hands, watching every move she made, but what struck him most was how uncommonly *still* she was. She didn't fidget or play with her chips, or look around at the other players. She peeked once at her down card, then didn't touch it again, signaling for another hit by tapping a fingernail on the table. Just because she didn't seem to be paying attention to the other players, though, didn't mean she was as unaware as she seemed.

"What's her name?" Dante asked.

"Lorna Clay," replied his chief of security, Al Rayburn.
"At first I thought she was counting, but she doesn't pay enough attention."

"She's paying attention, all right," Dante murmured. "You just don't see her doing it." A card counter had to remember every card played. Supposedly counting cards was impossible with the number of decks used by the casinos, but there were those rare individuals who could calculate the odds even with multiple decks.

"I thought that, too," said Al. "But look at this piece of tape coming up. Someone she knows comes up to her and speaks, she looks around and starts chatting, completely misses the play of the people to her left—and doesn't look around even when the deal comes back to her, just taps that finger. And damn if she didn't win. Again."

Dante watched the tape, rewound it, watched it again. Then he watched it a third time. There had to be something he was missing, because he couldn't pick out a single giveaway.

"If she's cheating," Al said with something like respect, "she's the best I've ever seen."

"What does your gut say?"

Al scratched the side of his jaw, considering. Finally, he said, "If she isn't cheating, she's the luckiest person walking. She wins. Week in, week out, she wins. Never a huge amount, but I ran the numbers and she's into us for about five grand a week. Hell, boss, on her way out of the casino she'll stop by a slot machine, feed a dollar in and walk away with at least fifty. It's never the same machine, either. I've had her watched, I've had her followed, I've even looked for the same faces in the casino every time she's in here, and I can't find a common denominator."

"Is she here now?"

"She came in about half an hour ago. She's playing blackjack, as usual."

"Bring her to my office," Dante said, making a swift decision. "Don't make a scene."

"Got it," said Al, turning on his heel and leaving the security center.

Dante left, too, going up to his office. His face was calm. Normally he would leave it to Al to deal with a cheater, but he was curious. How was she doing it? There were a lot of bad cheaters, a few good ones, and every so often one would come along who was the stuff of which legends were made: the cheater who didn't get caught,

even when people were alert and the camera was on him—
or, in this case, her.

It was possible to simply be lucky, as most people
understood luck. Chance could turn a habitual loser into
a big-time winner. Casinos, in fact, thrived on that hope.
But luck itself wasn't habitual, and he knew that what
passed for luck was often something else: cheating. And
there was the other kind of luck, the kind he himself pos-
sessed, but it depended not on chance but on who and what
he was. He knew it was an innate power and not Dame
Fortune's erratic smile. Since power like his was rare, the
odds made it likely the woman he'd been watching was
merely a very clever cheat.

Her skill could provide her with a very good living, he
thought, doing some swift calculations in his head. Five
grand a week equaled $260,000 a year, and that was just
from his casino. She probably hit them all, careful to keep
the numbers relatively low so she stayed under the radar.

He wondered how long she'd been taking him, how
long she'd been winning a little here, a little there, before
Al noticed.

The curtains were open on the wall-to-wall window in
his office, giving the impression, when one first opened
the door, of stepping out onto a covered balcony. The
glazed window faced west, so he could catch the sunsets.
The sun was low now, the sky painted in purple and gold.
At his home in the mountains, most of the windows faced
east, affording him views of the sunrise. Something in him
needed both the greeting and the goodbye of the sun. He'd
always been drawn to sunlight, maybe because fire was
his element to call, to control.

He checked his internal time: four minutes until
sundown. Without checking the sunrise tables every day,

he knew exactly when the sun would slide behind the mountains. He didn't own an alarm clock. He didn't need one. He was so acutely attuned to the sun's position that he had only to check within himself to know the time. As for waking at a particular time, he was one of those people who could tell himself to wake at a certain time, and he did. That talent had nothing to do with being Raintree, so he didn't have to hide it; a lot of perfectly ordinary people had the same ability.

He had other talents and abilities, however, that did require careful shielding. The long days of summer instilled in him an almost sexual high, when he could feel contained power buzzing just beneath his skin. He had to be doubly careful not to cause candles to leap into flame just by his presence, or to start wildfires with a glance in the dry-as-tinder brush. He loved Reno; he didn't want to burn it down. He just felt so damn *alive* with all the sunshine pouring down that he wanted to let the energy pour through him instead of holding it inside.

This must be how his brother Gideon felt while pulling lightning, all that hot power searing through his muscles, his veins. They had this in common, the connection with raw power. All the members of the far-flung Raintree clan had some power, some heightened ability, but only members of the royal family could channel and control the earth's natural energies.

Dante wasn't just of the royal family, he was the Dranir, the leader of the entire clan. "Dranir" was synonymous with king, but the position he held wasn't ceremonial, it was one of sheer power. He was the oldest son of the previous Dranir, but he would have been passed over for the position if he hadn't also inherited the power to hold it.

Behind him came Al's distinctive knock on the door. The outer office was empty, Dante's secretary having gone home hours before. "Come in," he called, not turning from his view of the sunset.

The door opened, and Al said, "Mr. Raintree, this is Lorna Clay."

Dante turned and looked at the woman, all his senses on alert. The first thing he noticed was the vibrant color of her hair, a rich, dark red that encompassed a multitude of shades from copper to burgundy. The warm amber light danced along the iridescent strands, and he felt a hard tug of sheer lust in his gut. Looking at her hair was almost like looking at fire, and he had the same reaction.

The second thing he noticed was that she was spitting mad.

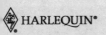

REQUEST YOUR FREE BOOKS!

2 FREE NOVELS PLUS 2 FREE GIFTS!

HARLEQUIN®

Blaze®

Red-hot reads!

YES! Please send me 2 FREE Harlequin® Blaze® novels and my 2 FREE gifts. After receiving them, if I don't wish to receive any more books, I can return the shipping statement marked "cancel." If I don't cancel, I will receive 6 brand-new novels every month and be billed just $3.99 per book in the U.S., or $4.47 per book in Canada, plus 25¢ shipping and handling per book and applicable taxes, if any*. That's a savings of at least 15% off the cover price! I understand that accepting the 2 free books and gifts places me under no obligation to buy anything. I can always return a shipment and cancel at any time. Even if I never buy another book from Harlequin, the two free books and gifts are mine to keep forever.

151 HDN EF3W   351 HDN EF3X

Name	(PLEASE PRINT)	
Address		Apt.
City	State/Prov.	Zip/Postal Code

Signature (if under 18, a parent or guardian must sign)

Mail to the **Harlequin Reader Service®:**
IN U.S.A.: P.O. Box 1867, Buffalo, NY 14240-1867
IN CANADA: P.O. Box 609, Fort Erie, Ontario L2A 5X3

Not valid to current Harlequin Blaze subscribers.

Want to try two free books from another line?
Call 1-800-873-8635 or visit www.morefreebooks.com.

* Terms and prices subject to change without notice. NY residents add applicable sales tax. Canadian residents will be charged applicable provincial taxes and GST. This offer is limited to one order per household. All orders subject to approval. Credit or debit balances in a customer's account(s) may be offset by any other outstanding balance owed by or to the customer. Please allow 4 to 6 weeks for delivery.

Your Privacy: Harlequin is committed to protecting your privacy. Our Privacy Policy is available online at www.eHarlequin.com or upon request from the Reader Service. From time to time we make our lists of customers available to reputable firms who may have a product or service of interest to you. If you would prefer we not share your name and address, please check here. ☐

HB07

HARLEQUIN®
Blaze™

COMING NEXT MONTH

#321 BEYOND SEDUCTION Kathleen O'Reilly
The Red Choo Diaries, Bk. 3
The last thing respected talk-show host Sam Porter wants is to be the subject of a sex blog—but that's exactly what happens when up-and-coming writer Mercedes Brooks gets hold of him…and never wants to let him go!

#322 THE EX-GIRLFRIENDS' CLUB Rhonda Nelson
Ben Wilder is stunned when he discovers a Web site dedicated to bashing him. Sure, he's a little wild. So what? Then he learns Eden Rutherford, his first love, is behind the site, and decides some payback is in order. And he's going to start by showing Eden *exactly* what she's been missing….

#323 THE MAN TAMER Cindi Myers
It's All About Attitude…
Can't get your man to behave? Columnist Rachel Westover has the answer: man taming, aka behavior modification. Too bad she can't get Garret Kelly to obey. Sure, he's hers to command between the sheets, but outside…well, there might be something to be said for going wild!

#324 DOUBLE DARE Tawny Weber
Audra Walker is the ultimate bad girl. And to prove it, she takes a friend's dare—to hit on the next guy who comes through the door of the bar. Lucky for her, the guy's a definite hottie. Too bad he's also a cop….

#325 KISS AND DWELL Kelley St. John
The Sexth Sense, Bk. 1
Monique Vicknair has a secret—she and her family are mediums, charged with the job of helping lost souls cross over. But when Monique discovers her next assignment is sexy Ryan Chappelle, the last thing she wants to do is send him away. Because Ryan is way too much man to be a ghost….

#326 HOT FOR HIM Sarah Mayberry
Secret Lives of Daytime Divas, Bk. 3
Beating her rival for a coveted award has put Claudia Dostis on top. But when Leandro Mandalor challenges her to address the sizzle between them, her pride won't let her back down. In this battle for supremacy the gloves—and a lot of other clothes—are coming off!

www.eHarlequin.com

HBCNM0407